INVISIBLE KITTIES

INVISIBLE KITTIES

WRITTEN AND ILLUSTRATED
BY YU YOYO

TRANSLATED FROM THE CHINESE
BY JEREMY TIANG

4th ESTATE · *London*

A FELINE STUDY OF FLUID MECHANICS

OR

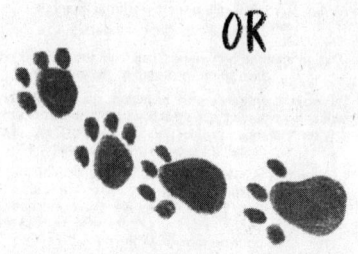

THE SPURIOUS INCIDENTS OF THE CATS IN THE NIGHT-TIME

4th Estate
An imprint of HarperCollins*Publishers*
1 London Bridge Street
London SE1 9GF

www.4thestate.co.uk

HarperCollins*Publishers*
Macken House, 39/40 Mayor Street Upper
Dublin 1, D01 C9W8, Ireland

First published in Great Britain in 2024 by 4th Estate
First published in the United States by HarperVia, an imprint of
HarperCollins*Publishers* in 2024
Originally published as 乌有猫 in China in 2021 by Yuefu Culture

1

Fiction

Copyright © Yu Yoyo 2021
English Translation © Jeremy J. Samuel 2024

Yu Yoyo asserts the moral right to be identified
as the author of this work in accordance with the
Copyright, Designs and Patents Act 1988

A catalogue record for this book is
available from the British Library

ISBN 978-0-00-871930-2

Design adapted by Yvonne Chan from the Chinese edition
Illustrations provided by the author

This novel is entirely a work of fiction. The names, characters
and incidents portrayed in it are the work of the author's imagination.
Any resemblance to actual persons, living or dead, events or
localities is entirely coincidental.

All rights reserved. No part of this publication may be
reproduced, stored in a retrieval system, or transmitted,
in any form or by any means, electronic, mechanical,
photocopying, recording or otherwise, without the
prior permission of the publishers.

This book is sold subject to the condition that it shall not, by
way of trade or otherwise, be lent, re-sold, hired out or otherwise
circulated without the publisher's prior consent in any form of
binding or cover other than that in which it is published and
without a similar condition including this condition being
imposed on the subsequent purchaser.

Set in Dante MT Std
Printed and bound in India by
Replika Press Pvt. Ltd.

MIX
Paper | Supporting
responsible forestry
FSC™ C016779

This book contains FSC™ certified paper and other controlled
sources to ensure responsible forest management.

For more information visit: www.harpercollins.co.uk/green

Contents

1. Ten Thousand Drops of Cat Rain — 1
2. Dream Cat — 5
3. Plant Cats, Get Cats — 9
4. Cat Picking — 14
5. New Flat — 18
6. Fat Cat — 23
7. Circles — 27
8. Invisible Kitties — 31
9. Marbles — 35
10. Clean Cat — 39

11. Catfall — 43

12. Boiling Cat — 47

13. Cat Hugging — 51

14. Private Property — 56

15. Gaseous Cat — 60

16. Dreaming — 63

17. Twilight Cat — 68

18. Flying — 72

19. Cat Ears — 77

20. Cat-and-Seek — 82

21. A Catlike Woman — 87

22. Black Cloud — 91

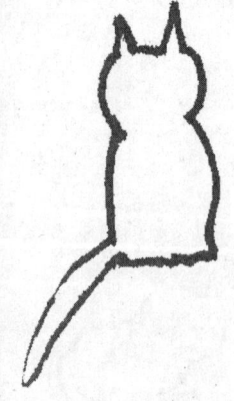

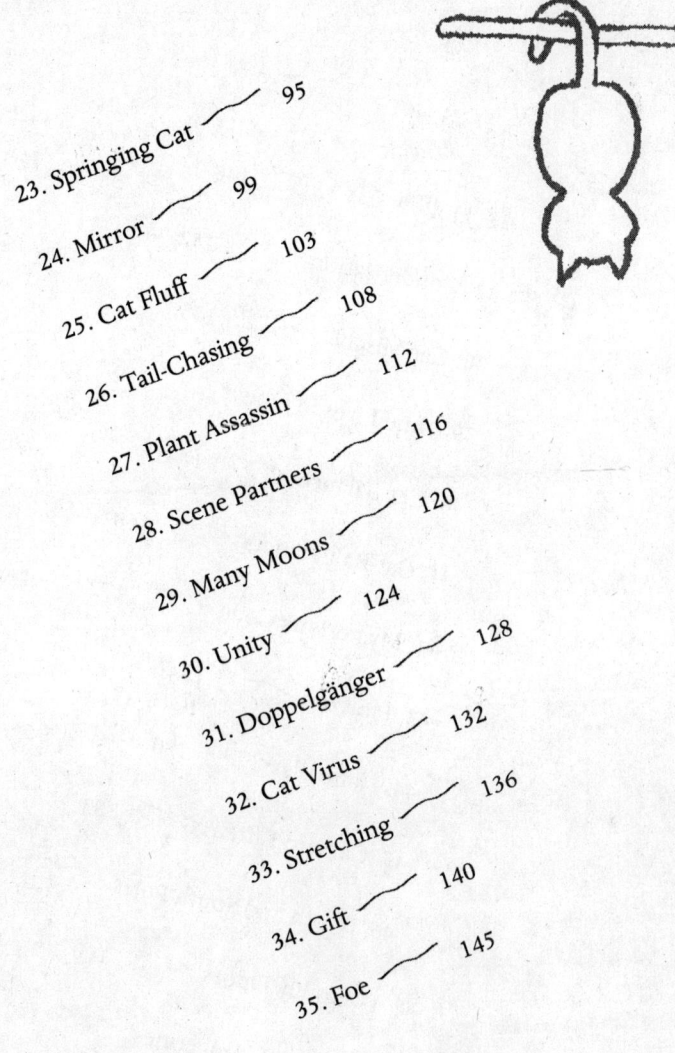

23. Springing Cat — 95
24. Mirror — 99
25. Cat Fluff — 103
26. Tail-Chasing — 108
27. Plant Assassin — 112
28. Scene Partners — 116
29. Many Moons — 120
30. Unity — 124
31. Doppelgänger — 128
32. Cat Virus — 132
33. Stretching — 136
34. Gift — 140
35. Foe — 145

36. Hollow Cat — 148
37. Condensation — 152
38. Cat Mischief — 155
39. Nine Lives in One — 159
40. Cat Balance — 164
41. Cat-Ball Planets — 168
42. Mysterious Code — 172
43. Horizon — 176
44. Hairballs — 180
45. Cat and Kitten — 183
46. North and South Poles — 186
47. Bodily Odors — 190
48. Fort of Tangerines — 193
49. Alarm Clock — 196

50. Dissolving — 199

51. Picking Mushrooms — 202

52. Catsup — 206

53. Extreme Sports — 209

54. Massage Parlor — 212

55. Stuck — 216

56. Blossoming — 219

57. Filtered — 222

58. Cats Are Gods — 225

59. Pillow and Blanket — 228

60. Two People, Two Cats — 231

Translator's ~~Note~~ Cat — 235

About the Author — 237

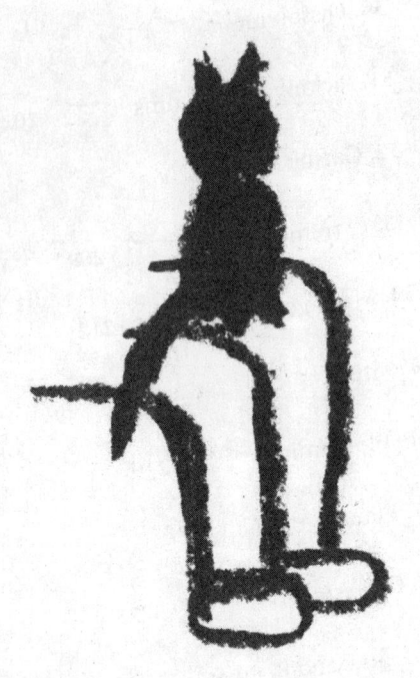

1
Ten Thousand Drops of Cat Rain

The cats required a curtain raiser before coming onstage—they would never so much as make an appearance without a bit of fanfare. Ahead of the rain came a little wind, only a smidge, like the sudden lurch of missing your footing on the stairs. Not too much force, no strong gusts, everything just a little askew. The kitties needed to hold back some of their energy for play.

The wind rose, and the kitties took advantage of the occasion to burrow into the shadowy clouds, concealing themselves behind the curtain. Amped up and full of excitement, ears dancing like beams of light, they darted here and there, countless glowing specks, riding the clouds toward the stage.

The stage in question was directly overhead, a patch of sky, neither near nor far. Look up and it would seem to be right there, but try to touch it and you'd soon realize it was out of reach. Such a gigantic swath of sky, I could have walked anywhere and still remained within its ambit. Dark clouds wafted closer, the curtain rustled open, and an unmissable performance began.

The kitties had set the stage for a grand presentation of cat rain, ten thousand drops in all.

From a distance, I watched the cats soaring ahead atop their clouds, fast as galloping horses. People saw this and hastened indoors, heads lifted to the sky. I happened to meet a cat's eyes with a flash of recognition but couldn't recall where we'd met before.

All this was back before I had a cat, before I had any idea where cats came from. The sky grew darker, the clouds lowered, and an urgent wind filled the building, foretelling a bout of cat rain. An abrupt *pitter patter pitter patter*. The show began in a flurry, no warning, no prologue. In the blink of an eye, every cat plummeted in raindrop form. *Splish splosh splash*. All done in a few seconds.

No one had time to react. It felt as if the storm had ended before it began.

The shortest downpour of this rainy season, so brief I barely got wet. I wished I'd been closer to center stage so I could have gotten a closer look at the cat rain.

Ten thousand drops of cat rain mean ten thousand kitties. Rain from the cats, cats in the rain. Cats and rain, one and the same. The cat rain vanished as it plopped onto the ground, leaving behind countless paw prints.

2
Dream Cat

The air was cool after the cat rain. I slept soundly that night.

I dreamed of a cat tunneling out of my ear, expanding all the while, faster than the eye could see. Dark-brown fur with scattered strands of gold. In the dream, I called him Doughball.

Doughball and I got on right away. He didn't show any fear and kept pulling pranks on me. His expansion was out of control, and for a while, I was worried he would grow too large for the room to contain him. Could Doughball's belly, round as it was, be filled with some kind of gas? I thought of pricking it with a needle to see if it would deflate but couldn't bring myself to. After all, when I stroked

Doughball, he was a flesh-and-blood cat—I didn't want to hurt him. And so I just let him inflate, bouncing around like a rubber ball.

Each day, Doughball went through his repertoire of tricks: flying leaps, high jumps, tail-biting, chasing himself. He was a springy thing, and I kept failing to catch him. Trying to make him stop, I had to chase him around the entire flat, jumping up and down like a monkey.

Doughball reached the size of a television and abruptly stopped growing. I put my hand to my chest and let out a sigh of relief. *Phew*.

Even though Doughball was no longer expanding, he was still several times the size of a regular cat and ate an extravagant amount. Our household expenses soared thanks to the bottomless pit that was his stomach. Husband grumbled that his wages were all going to Doughball. Yet when Doughball had eaten his fill and lay next to Husband, legs flopping in every direction, Husband was so delighted he couldn't stop beaming. *So cute*, he would murmur, forgetting his grievance.

Doughball scampered around in front of me each day, his frolicking as entertaining as any TV program. Husband and I had fallen out of the habit of watching television

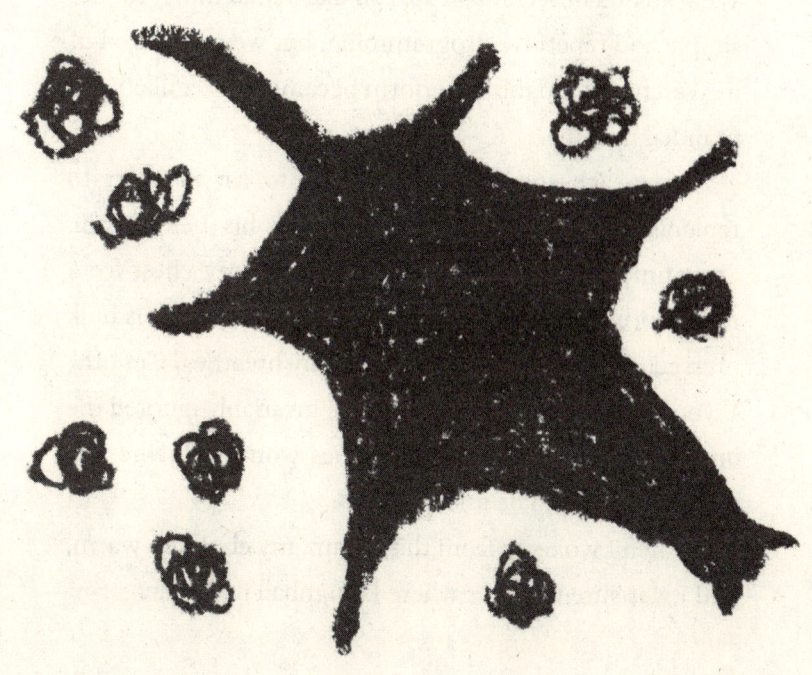

several years ago, but Doughball made us remember what it was like to settle down together in front of a show. Every episode was directed and performed by Doughball. We watched him climb, leap, run like a mad thing. Rather simple and repetitive programming, but we never tired of it. Watching Doughball perform became our regular postprandial pastime.

After each show, Doughball had to eat in order to replenish his strength and round out his belly again. Sometimes he would then nestle against my chest for a nap, snoring loudly. I enjoyed our snuggling, but his bulk pressed down on me till I could hardly breathe. "Get off," I would say. "You're too heavy!" He invariably ignored me and stayed put, though I sometimes wondered if he was just pretending to be asleep.

When I woke up from this dream, my chest felt warm, and I was sure that was where Doughball had been.

3
Plant Cats, Get Cats

I never used to pay much attention to cats as a species—you could say I lacked an understanding of them. Then Doughball began visiting me in my dreams, and though our time together was brief, it was enough to cultivate a feline appreciation within me. I didn't want to leave Doughball, but dreams didn't come every day, and he wasn't always in them.

The day came that I realized I hadn't dreamt of Doughball for a while and missed him very much. Whenever I ventured out, I couldn't stop myself from scouring trees and bushes, hoping a cat would pop out, even though I knew it wouldn't be Doughball.

Once I started seeking out cats, I naturally saw many

of them. It turned out there were plenty of kitties on the ground: in flower beds, in the mud, in fields, beneath trees. . . . They were everywhere, sauntering around in vast numbers, as if they had sprung from the earth itself.

Kitties are like any other vegetable. Plant melons, get melons. Plant beans, get beans. Plant cats, get cats.

In this world, there are those who plant cats, and those who pick them.

The cat planters have only to scatter cat seeds on the soil. No need for watering, fertilizing, or tending. Come spring, there'll be a harvest of countless kitties. And it's true—when spring arrives, the number of cats increases overnight. Once they've squirmed from the soil, they mature quickly.

Spring is cat-harvest time, the best season to pick them.

The springtime sun grows more plentiful each passing day. Cats emerge, alongside all of nature, as they return to life and everything is renewed, with no distinction between house cats and strays. They've all just gained consciousness and are now accepting their lives as cats.

The kitties stretch out their tiny paws and gingerly

probe the warmth of the sun. Side by side, they sprawl out on the fuzzy carpet of the earth. In good weather, you'll see cats energetically opening themselves up and lying flat to soak up the sunlight. When they've absorbed their fill, they'll slowly open their eyes.

When the cats sense they've ripened, they'll pluck themselves completely free of the soil. With all four feet on the ground, they'll take a few experimental steps on the earth's surface, then ramp it up until their legs are springing, fully extended, leaping ahead, sprinting.

Fresh from the soil, the cats dash swiftly in all directions. Some linger in the woods, others reach the road. You'll often notice cats emerging onto the street. Some fear people and hide, vanishing in a puff of smoke. Others, like Doughball, are mature enough to parade themselves in front of passersby as if to say, *Take me with you, take me away from here!* Cat lovers pause and bend down to stroke these cats, perhaps play with them for a while, or else head to a nearby convenience store to buy some cat treats. Sometimes the cats trail these humans a little ways and only stop if they don't look back.

Then there are cats who like people but don't wish to leave the soil, and so choose to sprout in a place where humans gather. They learn where and when cat lovers will bring them food and water. Now that they can wander freely without needing to go hungry, these cats linger outdoors forevermore, fostering a close connection to the earth, just as many people cling tightly to their hometowns.

4
Cat Picking

Having cycled through spring, summer, autumn, and winter, upon returning to spring the following year, I abruptly realized I was a person without a cat, a startling discovery.

Why didn't I have a cat? The question utterly stumped me. I chewed it over from morning to night, at home and out, while eating a meal or strolling down the street, but I couldn't come up with a satisfactory answer.

Many ideas just pop up in our heads, and there's no way to explain them. Some are passing fancies, which lead to endless weariness and regret. I didn't want to be one of those people. After all, cats are living things and must be taken seriously. They need to be understood, the way I understood Doughball.

I kept pondering and pondering every second of the day, so consumed I lost my way. As my eyes faded out of focus and the world before me blurred, a gray-white clump wafted before me. I rubbed my eyes, but there it remained. Stepping forward, I took a closer look and almost cried out. It was a stripy dark-gray cat, eyes shut, sound asleep. I clapped a hand over my gaping mouth.

A delicate little kitten, probably born not long ago, round face with slightly puffy cheeks, fur so soft and clean he couldn't be a stray. He was neither on the ground nor up a tree but suspended in midair, bobbing there quietly like a helium balloon, neither high nor low, close enough that I could reach out and pull him into my embrace.

I hugged the kitten, who remained sound asleep. I stroked his fur and gently kneaded his tiny ears, then rubbed his little claws, quietly inquiring, "And what's your name? Where do you come from?"

The cat remained fast asleep. I jogged home with him in my arms, hunched over for fear of dropping him. As I opened my front door, his eyelids drifted open but he remained motionless, gazing innocently at me, not showing the least bit of fear.

I went to the kitchen to pour him some milk and watched him lap the bowl dry looking perfectly content. He must have been starving. I fashioned a nest of blankets for him to sleep in with water and dry food nearby. When I turned around, he was curled up between the sofa cushions and had already dozed off. Only now did I understand, as if I'd just awoken from a dream, that there was a cat in my home. All of this happened with such inevitability that I didn't find any of it odd, and nor did Husband when he came home and saw the kitten. It was as if Cat had always been here.

Husband said he didn't look like he had come from out of the cat rain, nor did he seem to have grown from the soil. Rather, this was a cat who had been imagined into being and was now real.

Whether Cat had come from my mind or elsewhere, the truth was inescapable: I was now a person who had a cat. An actual cat. As for why I hadn't had a cat before this, the question no longer seemed important.

5
New Flat

Husband and I inhabit a small two-bedroom flat, just the right size for a couple. We're on such a high floor that when we look up from the ground, our home is a tiny dot no larger than a peanut, a particle of dirt flung into the sky. This minuscule speck is more than enough for me. Apart from accommodating me and Husband, it holds our wardrobes, chairs, sofas, bed, and many, many more miscellaneous items, cramming it full. And now, without any effort, we'd thrown a cat in there too. What an obliging little dot!

Day by day, the kitten grew used to his new surroundings. Having made the rounds and explored every corner, he declared dominion over all he surveyed. He lay wherever he wanted, including on Husband and me, incorporating us into his territory too.

Soon, Cat had occupied every space in the flat, which didn't seem smaller as a result but rather increased in size. And the expanding part was Cat himself.

Cat was a new flat within this old flat, a tiny dwelling within our already small one. Living with a cat is like living within a cat: no matter what's happening outside, you won't necessarily notice. The cat flat contained only the cat and nothing else, not even memory. I would often forget I was cooking, until the stench of the scorched pan reminded me. Right up to that point, I'd have been playing with the kitty, lavishing him with all my attention—waving a wand to make him dart around and leap into the air thoroughly revved up.

I clung greedily to every moment in the cat flat, not just because I wanted to spend more time on kitty games but also because its walls were velvety fur, and I could run my hands across them this way and that—*so smooth*—while Cat's soft *purr purr purrs* were broadcast right into my ears, as if the cat flat contained a surround sound system, cocooning me in tranquility.

The floor of the cat flat consisted of fleshy paw pads,

pink and tender, perfectly springy and softer than any carpet, more shock absorbent than any floorboard, more anti-slip than any tile. They yielded gently with each step, then sprang back instantly.

The only windows were Cat's eyes. Peering through them, you'd glimpse a cavernous hollow in his body, now dark and now light, mysterious and unpredictable. The space stretched beyond the bounds of my vision, reaching even farther than when I stood at the top of my building gazing at the sprawling city. There were no borders in sight, and unlike the city, the space was not crammed full of apartment blocks, car-filled roads, and heaving crowds.

What an endlessly changing world. One moment it darkened, turning into a vast cave in which nothing could be seen, threatening to swallow everything, so I clung tightly to the floorboards, terrified of being sucked into the blackness. Finally, a glimmer of light would appear, and only in its reassuring glow would I let out a sigh of relief. Just like that, the space would transform into a resplendent paradise. Here were swings, parallel bars, spiral slides, seesaws, and across the uneven ground were glossy green wheatgrass and fluttering butterflies for Cat to chase. He sprinted back and forth, over and under, blissfully happy. I

wanted to be in this vibrant wonderland too but couldn't find an entrance, so I had to watch from outside as Cat lived his best life, completely at ease. I gazed, mesmerized, as the light dimmed, until the playground disappeared and all I could see was myself in the glass with longing in my eyes for that extinguished idyll. My heart could be seen in the reflection too, thumping steadily, and if I listened closely, I could hear a clear echo.

6
Fat Cat

When Cat first came to live with us, he was so scrawny that a gust of wind could have toppled him over, and Husband was able to lift him in one hand. He proved to have an astonishing appetite though, polishing off prodigious quantities each day. All his portions and some of mine. Whenever he saw me with food in hand, he would plop in front of me, calling *meow meow*, butting my arm till I didn't know whether to go on eating or not. With his cuteness, he kidnapped me; with his mischief, he tricked me into funneling him extra food and drink, easily liberating me of my snacks. If you set everything Cat ate end to end, it would stretch as long as an entire train, a different carriage for each kind of food, ferrying all sorts of nutrition.

Having eaten a train, Cat's body also grew very long, stretching all the way from the balcony through the living room into the bedroom. If we had more rooms, I'm sure he could have gotten even longer. Cat often conducted this train through our flat, hauling his long body behind him. *Choo choo* this way, *choo choo* back the other, as if he were chasing something, or maybe being chased. Often I would see his legs in one room and his head in another.

As Cat's appetite increased, so his body continued elongating. He could loop himself over the laundry rack several times, swinging back and forth. He taught himself to swing, being both swing and swinger in one. After every meal, with nothing left to do, Cat would hang himself up and swing freely, frittering away his time.

I was now dedicating much more time to petting Cat. Each head-to-tail stroke used to last just a few seconds, but now it took several minutes to get from one end to the other, quite a workout. Cat didn't always stretch out but enjoyed napping with his body twisted this way and that, or coiled around a table leg. For a proper petting, I needed to weave in and out too, moving from one room to another.

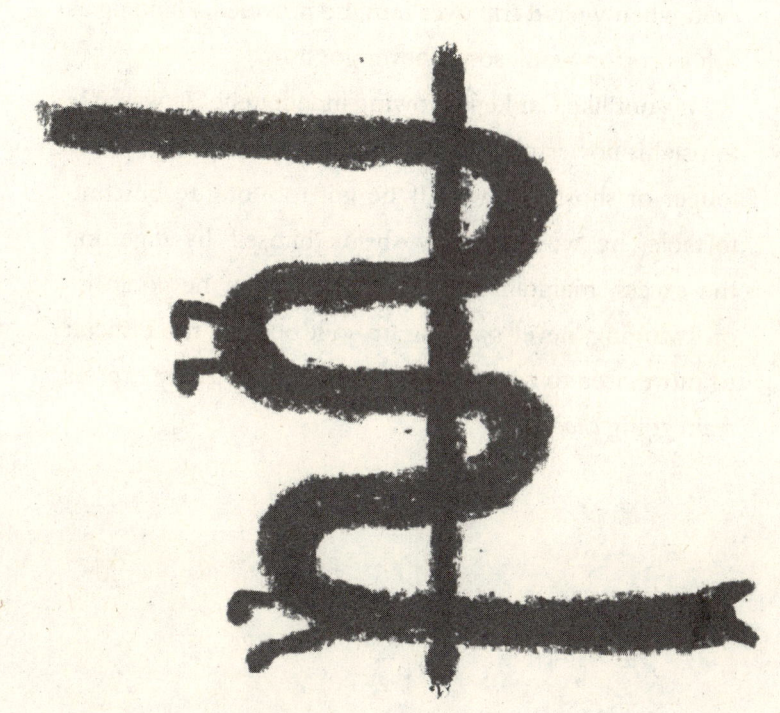

Even with his new, longer body, Cat didn't bring any trouble into our lives. His body was everywhere at once, splayed in all directions, but too soft to get in our way. And even when we did trip over him, he provided a landing as soft as cotton wool, so we never got hurt.

It's not like Cat kept growing indefinitely. He was able to use his powerful digestion to tailor his length, growing longer or shorter at will. If he got too long to be comfortable, he would simply shrink himself by digesting the excess, maintaining his size. This way, he could go on swinging, never swelling up so it became too difficult to move, free to continue running around, a tiny express train going *choo choo*.

7
Circles

All around our home, Cat draws countless circles of all sizes.

Many are concentric, larger circles around smaller ones, some stacked like raindrop ripples on water, round after round, too many to number, pressed tightly together or overlapping, slowly spreading, then vanishing. These are all invisible, undetectable to the human eye, felt rather than seen. These circles arrive stealthily. If either of us moves, Cat draws a new circle. Every step I take is from one circle to the next.

Cat draws these circles not with compasses, not by tracing around ring-shaped objects, but simply by maintaining a fixed distance from me so this length becomes

the radius of a circle. He creates round after round, like the monkey king drawing magic rings on the ground with his golden staff, trapping the priest and his fellow disciples within. Cat's circles aren't quite the same, of course. The monkey king drew rings to keep demons at bay, whereas Cat's repel nothing. They fail to separate me from him and don't protect me in any way.

When Cat encloses me and himself in the same circle, it's because he wants us to share a defined space. This space could be vast or claustrophobic—that's entirely dependent on the distance between us. When we are far apart, the cat circle grows large, while a small round is fine for when I'm close by. When I'm at one end of a room and Cat is at the other, the resultant circle is larger than the apartment itself, arcing beyond the perimeter of our property, and when sunlight passes through, it splits into seven colors: red, orange, yellow, green, blue, indigo, violet, a glory of hues reaching into the sky. Through the window, Cat and I look upon the rainbow we've created.

No matter how often my position relative to Cat's changes, we remain within the same circle. No matter where I go, Cat places me at the center. As long as Cat and I share a circle, even when I'm focused on my own work and ignoring him, Cat remains calm and at ease. I never need to worry about him. Every now and then, I glance in his direction. We don't bother each other. There are no restrictions apart from that boundary. I've come to feel as free living with Cat as if those circles didn't exist at all.

One time, I suddenly had the strong sense that the circle had disappeared. That was strange—had Cat forgotten to draw one? Just as I was getting puzzled, I looked down and realized he was asleep on my lap.

8

Invisible Kitties

Soon after we acquired Cat, he abruptly whittled away into nothingness, as if he hadn't existed at all. The presence of Cat in our home became as subtle as air.

When breathing in the air we cannot see, we also inhale Cat. Cat is the air itself.

There have been many times when I couldn't find Cat anywhere, and no matter how I searched, he seemed to grow more hidden. When no one's paying attention, Cat stretches out his limbs, extending them to such lengths that his body grows impossibly thin, his fur getting paler, until he's completely transparent, melting into the air. See-through Cat is in the dark, while I stand in full light. He can see me, but I can't see him. That's not very fair, I grumble, but there's nothing to be done, you can't talk fairness with cats, you can only blame yourself for not being able to metamorphose in the same way.

Countless times, I have ransacked the entire apartment, getting increasingly panicky, only to turn and find him crouched at my feet, leaning forward as if he were joining me in the hunt. At these moments, resentment builds up inside me. Why do I waste my time searching? Is anyone as pathetic as me?

Cat follows me into every room, accompanying me in my search for him, and not once do I notice his presence. Cats can turn themselves invisible, not making a sound as they pad along beside you. Cat paws are so very light and come with fleshy pads that muffle their steps, eradicating any noise, or perhaps absorbing it into the softness. When a kitty lifts their leg or leaps, the sound is whisked away too and never reaches human ears.

Even when I know Cat is somewhere in the room, I can't catch any sign of him, just as I understand that air surrounds us at all times, but whenever I reach out for it, my hands close on nothingness. Cat uses the transparency of air to turn himself see-through, concealing himself in

vapor, melting his body into nothingness. Invisibility is a cloak that Cat drapes over himself.

If you want a cat to show himself, you can't pay too much attention.

Cats appear when they unwittingly glisten, a halo of light. Cat's front and rear halves are generally separated, so we can't see him in his entirety, which also makes it hard to determine his actual location. Different parts of Cat are quartered across various areas of the apartment, and when one of them discloses a gleam, it manifests as a dazzle of confusion to human eyes.

And yet I have to keep the faith that Cat will eventually show up, but there's no way to predict the time or place nor will there be a concrete reason. Whenever I can't find Cat, he voluntarily reveals himself. When he pads up to me and stares at me with his penetrating eyes, everything seems more real than before, as if he has never been gone. Facing off with me, Cat's gaze is sharp and icy, piercing right through my eyes, as if he wants to absorb all of me into himself, rendering me nonexistent.

9
Marbles

As a kid, I had a drawerful of marbles, which featured in games with my little playmates. We'd dig a small hole in the ground, place all our marbles into it, and lie prone in front of the hole. With utter focus, we'd hold our breaths and each shut one eye. The other eye would seek out the best angle, and with exactly the right amount of force, our thumbs would launch a single marble into the hole. Whoever knocked the most marbles out of the hole won the game.

A marble sent out in this way would knock against others with a *clink*, colorful orbs on the ground colliding, rolling, sparkling.

Mama didn't like me playing marbles. "How could a

girl lie on the ground like that?" she would complain. "It's filthy. Do you know how hard it is to scrub the dirt out of your clothes?" I paid no more attention to her words than the wind. They went in one ear and out the other—she might as well not have bothered speaking. Having tossed Mama's words to the back of my mind, I went out as usual to play, getting myself thoroughly grubby. By the time I was done, everything between my knees, chest, and elbows was blackened. When Mama saw me, she'd grind her teeth, biting back the urge to give me a good thrashing.

One evening, Mama told me a bedtime story in which the marbles that kids played with were actually kitty eyes. In the story, hunters would catch cats and gouge out their eyes, which were delivered to the owner of the local shop to be sold to us children.

This story terrified me, and I didn't sleep a wink that night. Whenever I shut my eyes, I saw countless blinded kitties, some of whom had retained a single eye, which was even more distressing. I trembled to think I hoarded a drawerful of cat eyes in my room. What if the cats they belonged to found their way to our home and demanded their eyes back? For several nights after that, I was so consumed by worry that I couldn't get to sleep.

From then on, I never dared play marbles again.

The way cat eyes roll around in their sockets does bring to mind the marbles I played with as a child, light shining through them, making them sparkle. Nowadays, when I think of Mama's story, I'm no longer scared. Cats are so mischievous it makes more sense to me that they'd be the ones stealing children's marbles to insert into their sockets.

Cat eyes swivel like marbles rolling across the ground. Having Cat in my life is like winning a couple of shiny new marbles.

These days, I often lie belly down on the floor, staring into Cat's eyes, and he stares back at me. When he rolls his eyes, I roll mine back at him. He blinks at me, and I do the same back. I shoot him a look in return for each of his, matching him blow for blow, flicking the pair of glass orbs back at him. My gaze and Cat's become a game of marbles. After several rounds, neither of us has lost, neither of us has won.

10
Clean Cat

Cat jumps onto my desk and stands amid untidy stacks of manuscripts, coolly scanning his surroundings. His eyes blaze bright as a torch, as if he can't wait to set this jumble on fire, burning it away to nothing, leaving just the pristine surface of the desk for him to proudly strut, curl up, or sprawl upon.

Cats love everything around them to be spotless and laid bare, a canvas against which they can strike all sorts of poses, stretching in any direction they like. Cat loathes my work desk because it is cluttered at all times with book manuscripts and other objects, an obstacle course. Crouched between piles of books, he furrows his brow and shoots an icy glare at me between the gaps of the debris, a chilling sight. A moment later, he shoves my ziggurats of books over, crashing them to the ground before I have a chance to catch them. Cat is well-practiced at this, and if I'm a moment too slow sticking out my arm to stop him, all I can do is watch as these towers disintegrate before my eyes like skyscrapers being demolished. With a smug air, Cat licks his murderous paws before swiftly fleeing the scene of the crime.

Cat often spirits away the erasers I leave on my desk, nudging them out of sight so they aren't there when I need them. Any item I don't put back in its place immediately after using it, Cat regards as fair game for confiscation. With a swift motion, the object is in his jaws—and once apprehended in this manner—will be extremely difficult to recover. The objects that Cat stashes are gone without a trace, and all I can do is wait for the distant day when they will reveal themselves. During our last spring cleaning, Husband reached under the sofa and emerged with several pencils, a few erasers, and a lighter.

I don't enjoy tidying up, while Cat is compulsively neat. Like a public health inspector, he paces up and down my desk all day long, forbidding me to leave anything out of place. I tense up, nervous that I might forget to put

something away. When I asked Husband what I should do about the headache of being surveilled by a cat all day long, he unexpectedly took Cat's side, and even volunteered to join Cat on cleanliness patrol. And so I, the slob, was left all alone.

If I'd known how this would turn out, I'd have never spoken to Husband to begin with. Not only have I lost a potential ally, I've gained a nemesis. From now on, I'll have to be much more careful, not daring to risk a moment's untidiness.

This has increased Husband's affection for our fastidious cat. Cat only has to wash his face or lick his fur for Husband to heap praise upon him. Cat daintily moistens a front paw, then rubs at his chin and the corners of his mouth, working from bottom to top, first the left side of his face and then the right, before moving on to the rest of his body, until his fur glistens. When Cat basks in the sun, the warmth of the rays emulsifies with calcium and saliva into a substance he spreads evenly over himself with his tongue, creating a translucent membrane of light. With this layer of protection, he's free to roll around on the floor as much as he likes. When he's done, a simple swipe of his tongue removes all the dust, restoring his shine once again.

11
Catfall

Night is a black canvas sack of infinite size and capacity, stealthily slipping over the entire world. Come nightfall, we are all people in the sack, and no one can escape. Everyone gets used to their new conditions, adapting to life in the sack, installing all manner of lamps in an attempt to restore daylight, but it's never quite as bright, and so life in the sack feels arid and dull, which is why we spend most of our time there sleeping.

Cats find themselves in the sack too, sometimes so quiet they seem to merge with the material, other times growing so rowdy you'd think they might tear a hole in the sack. As my husband and I lie in bed, we can clearly hear Cat's claws going *schwaa schwaa* in the living room, telling us he is sprinting from one end of the couch to the other, back and forth in a wild relay race. Luckily, Cat and I formed a tacit agreement early on: in the pitch-black night, even when my ears tell me what Cat is getting up to, no matter how much destruction is involved, I won't stop him. After all, his actions are invisible by night, and it's easy to pretend that what we do not see does not exist.

By day, Cat sleeps with all his might, for as long as he possibly can, and when he's finally had his fill, his body is replete with energy, which fuels him through the long night of activity in the black canvas sack, running around charting its dimensions. No one to date has figured out the measurements of this sack. Cat is trying his best to work it out, but its sheer size foils him, as does the short window of night. He can only explore a small section at a time, for the sack vanishes when daybreak arrives.

When darkness falls, Cat's headlights come on: two bright spots of green, one in each eye. Even when his surroundings are unilluminated, Cat sees everything and can navigate with confidence, doing whatever he wants. Cat observes all this not by lighting up his surroundings but simply by brightening his own eyes. Cat eyes are able to stay on till dawn, expending neither electricity nor bodily energy.

If Cat were to remain still, the sack would turn immensely huge in an instant. Instead, he switches on his eye-lights and walks around, leaping from place to place. Any object—a nail, a lighter, a pair of scissors—might get brushed against at any moment, and each item that Cat touches is a border of the sack. By groping around in the dark, Cat uses his own body to measure the size of the sack. Every scratch of the sofa, each overturning of a jar, every disturbance of my books—all of these are the result of Cat testing the limits of his confinement. The sack shrinks and expands at will. At its largest, it swallows everything in the whole world and still has room to spare. At its tiniest, it shrouds Cat tightly, molding to his skin, so each little move brings him up against its walls.

12
Boiling Cat

Cat often emits a gurgling rumble, like a little round kettle filled with water. Whenever I put my hand on his belly and rub it a few times, something quite miraculous happens.

Cat begins to boil water with a *purr purr purr*, as if my hand has turned on the gas, causing flames to leap in Cat's belly, heating the waterskin. In just a couple of seconds, the water boils and roils, filling with bubbles that rise to the surface.

With the water boiled, Cat shuts his eyes and drifts off into sleep, and the low rumble transitions to faint snoring. That's why he needs so much water inside him, to then emerge from the corner of his mouth as drool.

Rather than let all this scalding water go to waste, it's

best to pour it out and make yourself a drink, say coffee. It tastes just like normal, but the thing to remember is you'll need to relocate to a room temporarily unoccupied by Cat in order to enjoy it alone. Cat is very sensitive to smells, you see, and the faintest whiff of anything good to eat or drink will make him run in circles, pestering you endlessly.

Cat never boils water when he's by himself—that would be a waste. After all, he wouldn't be drinking it, he only drinks the water I pour him. Cat prefers running water and comes sprinting over whenever he hears gurgling from the faucet, stretching out his tongue to lap from it, *flik flik flik*, much more satisfying than drinking from a bowl.

The water that fills Cat's belly is for me: not just to boil and drink but also to warm my feet. I lower them into the basin of hot liquid, and little bubbles begin rising around my soles, the belches that Cat hasn't yet had a chance to let out. Actually, the water isn't essential—just putting my feet onto Cat's belly is enough to feel his warmth, and before too long, I'm all toasty.

Cat's belly never needs a refill, and the water never depletes or varies in quality. No matter what, it will never get used up. Dispense some, and the water level rises up to

where it originally was a moment later. Cat's insides are like an ancient well whose depths contain an inexhaustible supply of water.

Cat water boiling differs from a regular kettle, with steam escaping through the spout. With a cat, their bellies rise and fall rhythmically, as if something is squirming inside. Press your ear to Cat's side, and you'll clearly catch an unbroken rumble churning away. No wonder there's a ceaseless supply of water: he's sneakily installed a pump in there.

When the pump gets going, there's a *splish splosh* in Cat's belly as water gushes in and begins boiling, *purr purr purr*. Husband had a fright the first time he heard this noise—he thought Cat was angry about something and was about to attack him. He actually dropped Cat and ran away. Watching this, I burst out laughing, then gently informed Husband that the gurgling sound meant Cat was at his most comfortable and happiest.

Still a little wary, Husband brought his ear closer and listened, and sure enough, Cat even generously rolled over to expose his pure-white belly. Husband gently stroked it, and Cat began rumbling again. A thermos whose exterior is thirty-odd degrees, holding boiling water, never bubbling over or damaging the container through its heat.

13
Cat Hugging

Husband comes from the North, and whenever it gets to winter, he starts complaining how we don't have heating down South, so the cold cuts right to his bones as if the southern winter has gathered in his joints, icy winds and frosty air slipping right into his marrow, setting up an ice factory in there, enough to make you shiver.

Our flat is full of freezing air, and the wind seeps through every crevice. Husband huddles into a ball, his face ghastly pale, not uttering a sound. I hug Cat and sit next to Husband, neither of us saying a word. This little bit of cold is nothing to me. Soothed by my two-handed petting, Cat drifts off quietly, while heat slowly rises through my fingers, circulating through my body and thawing it until I gradually feel warm again. Cat lies perfectly still on my lap, like a hot-water bottle. Cat's body is blazing hot, and he transfers his warmth to me, chipping away at the iciness.

One time, I decided to pass Cat to Husband so he could warm up too. As I held Cat up, he swayed slightly and I heard the water in his belly slapping against his skin like ocean waves against the shore. Miraculous cat! From a kettle to a hot-water bottle. Those two objects might not seem very different, but a hot-water bottle is softer, more soothing. It makes you want to hold it and never let go.

Husband took Cat and hastily pressed his face into Cat's belly, stroking the fur along the grain. I watched as color returned to his face, and his grimace softened into a more natural expression.

Having been thawed by Cat, Husband was back to normal. I asked for Cat back, but it was too late. Husband refused. Clutching him tight in both hands, he kept me from stealing Cat away. He wanted the hot-water bottle all to himself.

Hug a cat and you'll get warm again. Even if you can't do that, letting a cat wander around your house is also a good way to disperse his heat into every corner.

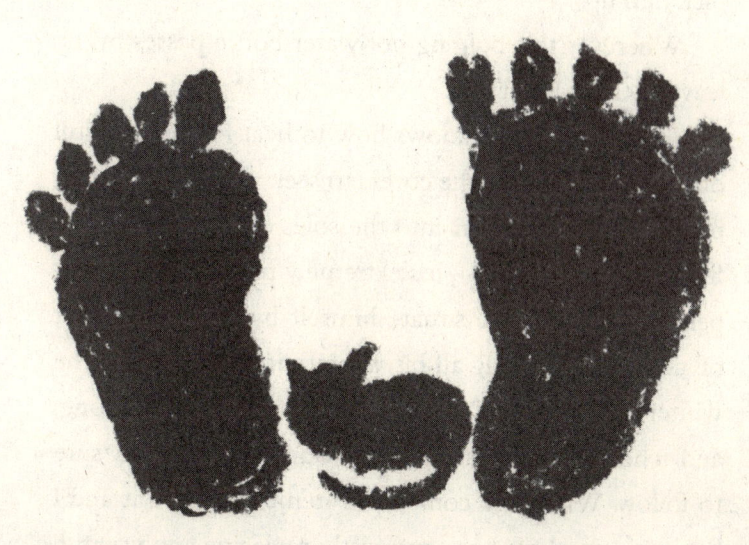

This mobile hot-water bottle never needs charging or refilling—the cat can simply use the kettle function to heat the water already stored in his body, *purr purr purr*, whenever anyone needs it, keeping it warm twenty-four seven, which is why a cat feels so toasty whenever you pick him up.

Wherever this bulging hot-water bottle passes by, he leaves a trail of warmth.

Even though Cat knows how to heat himself, he still often creeps beneath the covers to seek warmth from me, pressing his velvety fur into the soles of my feet. I don't find this ticklish at all—it's extremely pleasant. As it happens, Cat chooses to situate himself by the coldest part of my body, nuzzling all his warmth into my feet. In the winter particularly, Cat sleeps by my legs all night long, and when your feet are warm, your whole body is sure to follow. When I've come up to temperature, Cat and I begin passing heat back and forth, replacing any warmth lost from either of our bodies until we've reached equilibrium. And so in heating me, Cat doesn't lose any of his own warmth but actually ends up even cozier than before.

Cat burrows under the covers during daytime too and often naps there for the entire day. When I see a bump in the otherwise flat expanse of the bed, chances are good that there's a snoozing cat in there. If I lift the blanket, I'll find a curled-up feline who lazily shoots me a look, then shuts his eyes again. Slipping my hand between Cat and bed, I feel an instant jolt of toastiness. Sometimes I worry these high temperatures might roast Cat, but perhaps he arrived already roasted, and that's how he's able to remain so piping hot.

14
Private Property

We humans, well, we have lots of flaws: we tend to be full of ourselves and feel the need to affirm humankind's superiority. I'm no exception. Sometimes I foolishly try to annex Cat as my personal property. After all, I found Cat, I feed and water him, I scoop his poop. Therefore, I assume Cat is mine, which means he's obliged to obey me and submit to my instructions.

I give Cat orders as an "owner": *stay right here next to me, don't go anywhere, let me pet you.* I wake him when he's sound asleep, insisting he play with me right that moment. Cat is incapable of resisting because he doesn't have as much strength as a human and I can rouse him with a simple movement of my arm. He doesn't go along with this willingly though, and escapes at the first opportunity, or at least scowls at me. These are the few occasions Cat looks displeased with me, and my playfulness evaporates in an instant. I even feel a little ashamed at Cat's expression, which clearly says, "Hey, our games are a gift that *I* bestow upon *you*."

We must be delusional to think we could own cats.

Cat frequently ignores me, even when he's less than three feet away, right in front of me. I call his name over and over to no response except a slight extension of a front paw and a quizzical tilt of his head. When Cat settles into my chair, keeping me from my work, he pretends not to hear me shouting at him to scram, as if I'm no more than the empty air.

It's not just the chair—he occupies my pillow too, leaving me nowhere to sleep. I've now given in and placed a smaller pillow next to what has become Cat's perch. He snoozes by my head and sometimes kicks me in his sleep, waking me. He also takes up the mattress, the sofa, my desk, and my husband. Yes, Husband is his nesting place, and he enjoys lounging between Husband's thighs, mewling and acting cute. Husband gives him fingers to play with, teasing him, an entire human absorbed by catness.

When Cat drifts off, Husband doesn't dare move a muscle and only speaks in the tiniest of voices for fear of disturbing Cat.

As far as Cat is concerned, he's the head of the household, and he goes around taking up whatever space he likes, god forbid anyone offend him. Cat does not like to be hugged without his consent, and he has to be the one to initiate any embrace by walking up to you. All day long, he prances and rolls next to me and Husband in order to check on his property, making sure we're doing okay and still under his command.

In the unspoken tussle of wills with Cat, we have very much emerged in a weaker position. Husband has happily surrendered any authority he had to Cat. Now that Cat is calling the shots, Husband and I have switches installed in us. When Cat needs us, he appears—that's the only time we get to touch him. At other times, he's nowhere to be seen—but it's actually we who have disappeared, vaporized by Cat so he can enjoy some alone time. Then he gets hungry and flicks the switch, and I rush to pour him a heaping bowl of dry food. When he's eaten his fill, he flicks the switch again, dismissing me. I do everything I can to please Cat, bringing out his favorite foods to entice

him, trying to get into his good graces, making myself indispensable so he'll keep me around longer. Cat doesn't care though. He eats his fill, licks his chops, then swaggers away, flicking the switch. And with that, I vanish.

In the end, I'm just one of Cat's possessions.

Now that I'm private property, when I get home each day, Cat sniffs at me, inspecting me for unfamiliar odors. If he detects a whiff of another cat, I'll be in big trouble: he'll storm away in a huff and ignore me for a few days.

15
Gaseous Cat

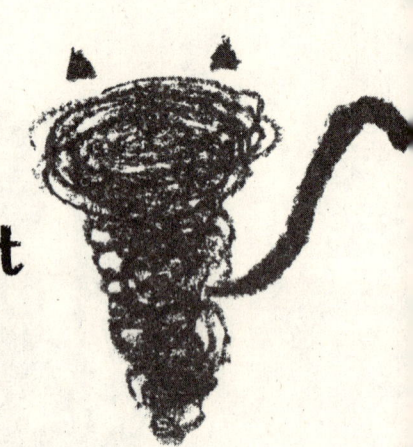

Cat is drawn to running water, not because he hopes to catch a glimpse of his own reflection but out of instinct—because he is inseparable from liquid. Indeed, he always vanishes quickly from my sight while the water continues gurgling away.

Cat trickles around bookshelves, beneath the breakfast bar, past my work desk, into our wardrobe, and under our bed. How can we be sure this is Cat? Because the stream eventually reaches me, and I feel my skin moisten where Cat has lapped at it. A tongue of water that dissolves me where it touches.

In the afternoon, Cat and I ripple through the flat together, drifting wherever the sunlight falls. Our soft bodies contort into all kinds of shapes and unseemly postures. Cat has always been more malleable than me, a skill I don't particularly envy.

Sometimes I morph into a huge container, a venue within which Cat can perform. He turns flat, then bulbous; thick, then slender; vast, then tiny; round, then pancakelike; a normal cat, then nothing at all.

Yes, Cat can induce himself to vanish.

Once, I went searching everywhere for him, from the living room to the kitchen, from the kitchen to the balcony, from the balcony to the bedroom, from the bedroom to the pool. I called his name, but cats answer to no name, and in the end they are all Meow Meow.

Meow Meow! Meow Meow!

Cat didn't respond. The sun blazed, pouring its light onto the name as I called. Shimmering circles appeared before my eyes. I clung to them and climbed through the air. Before too long, I reached the highest vantage in the entire city. The rings of light were made of seven colors, becoming transparent when they aligned. Such adorable see-through rounds. I stared at them and watched them grow faint.

Meow Meow! Meow Meow!

Cat appeared before me, and I couldn't wait to ask where he'd been. Then I noticed his fur was all ruffled and windswept, and understood: the rings of light had all been Cat. He'd gone from solid to liquid, then evaporated into gas. And now he had returned to his habitual state.

16
Dreaming

I often dream of cats, both the ones I know and strangers. Occasionally, they appear together, a diverse gathering. The number of cats is steadily increasing, and my dreams are getting so crowded that some cats are unable to squeeze in, or they do but I can never remember them afterward.

Fortunately, certain cats do linger in my memory. The dreams evaporate when I wake the next morning, but the cats stay on my mind, like actors remaining center stage even after the backdrop has been whisked away.

I can visualize these cats in minute detail and describe exactly what they did in my dream. When I tell Husband

I dreamed of cats again, he leans over and whispers in my ear that whatever we do, we mustn't let Cat hear of this.

Over and over, I dream of cats, but I don't know if Cat ever dreams of me. That's a question that I've held in my heart for a very long time. Finally, unable to dismiss it, I asked Husband if there was any way to find out. He said, "Why don't you ask Cat?" I replied, "If I could ask Cat, why would I bother asking *you*?" He retorted that I should pry open Cat's brain and have a look. I rolled my eyes and he laughed. He was joking, he said, then he proposed a possible solution, one that could be easily put into action at no one's expense.

Husband's idea was for me to fall asleep at the same time as Cat so our dreams would sync up. This way, we could share a dream, a larger one than either of us could individually muster, two dreams in one. Through these connected dreams, I would find passage into Cat's dreamworld and discover if I existed there. Cat and I could trade dreamscapes: he would be in my dream, and I in his.

I tried it out that very night.

I went to bed at the usual time, and Cat jumped in after

me. As usual, he slept on my old pillow, while I had my little pillow next to it. In order to make sure our dreams would be linked, I shifted Cat so his head touched mine. He didn't object.

Gently stroking Cat's fur, I listened for the *purr purr purr* that told me he had drifted off. The soft rumbling lulled me into sleep too.

At some point, I realized I could hear meowing. Looking around for the source of the sound, I spotted a cat I had never seen before. This new cat glanced at me, then bounded ahead, leading me down a long, dark tunnel, moving so fast I had to jog to keep up.

I can't be sure how far we went before I finally saw a speck of light up ahead—hopefully an exit. We continued jogging toward the light, but when we were almost there, the other cat abruptly vanished. My heart pounded, and I felt a flicker of fear—but the exit was close by, so I hurried. When I got there, I found a flat that looked exactly like mine. Inside was Husband in the middle of the big cleanup he did once a month. As he toiled, he grumbled that Cat had taken a foot-long shit on his computer keyboard.

I searched all around, but the other cat had utterly vanished. Out of nowhere, a voice behind me shouted, "Hey, what are you doing over there? What do you think you're looking at?" Startled, I spun around, but no one was there. Even Husband had disappeared. But there was the other cat, crouched by the computer, smiling icily at me.

17
Twilight Cat

Twilight begins the epilogue of the day, the sky's brilliance calibrated for human eyes, no longer dazzling. At this time, the entire weight of dusk falls onto Cat's belly. This isn't too heavy—in fact, Cat rolls over to show his underside, willingly accepting the burden.

Having napped for hours, Cat has absorbed an afternoon's worth of sun, storing all that warmth in his belly. It is the greatest treasure of any cat, glittering like gold. All of this treasure, Cat now exchanges, for a skein of orange-pink, twilight hues. This loose, springy radiance assumes the exact same texture as cat fur.

The sun has been all but exhausted through the course of the day. Very little remains of it at this point, just some shards propped up by clouds. Fragments of sun are descending all around, flaking into countless crimson streaks.

Cat successfully lures these remnants of star into the room. There, he grinds them into even finer crystalline particles, which he silently spreads across the floor, forming unorthodox geometric figures. Cat enjoys dozing among these mosaics, which, warmer than the bare floor, become a sort of carpet. They carry the heat of the sun within them, pulverized into atoms, too small to be seen. Cat sprawls among them, reaching a lazy paw into every shape, framed by these shapes, yet remaining unbounded. These pieces of sun reach over cat's body too, blanketlike.

Twilight descends, shifting the shapes, and Cat adjusts his posture with them.

Cat is always whetting his claws so that when the sun begins to set, he can scratch minuscule tears in the sky where solar heat can accumulate. Some days, there are more tears than others, some days, they are farther away, a vague intimation, exactly right for cat's personality. Cat understands that the world is spinning, and so the sun will reappear day after day. He has many opportunities to see the twilight, each of them equally valuable.

So how to make each dusk feel special, different from

the previous ones? At some point, Cat seems to have made a decision to find something unique in every one of these completely mundane twilights.

When he's in a good mood, Cat can drag the twilight out by as much as nine yards so the sun is forced to compensate, descending the same distance below the horizon. That night is therefore shortened by the whole nine yards, though how much time that translates to only Cat can say.

Cat does everything for the sake of me and Husband,

to ensure we get home before dark. If we stay out longer, sunset is delayed; if we get back early, dusk hastens. While waiting for us to return, Cat does his best to hold on to the patterns of twilight, giving us time to change into slippers and step across the shapes he's arranged for us.

Even if these mosaics have vanished, that doesn't matter—Cat has already gouged holes in the air, and as long as they remain there, so does the heat they contain. No matter how late we get home, we can still feel the lingering warmth of twilight in the flat.

And if we happen to reach home just at the moment of sunset, that's the happiest possible coincidence for Cat. He can display his painstaking creations at their very best, no need to wait for next time.

After that, Cat leaps into a human embrace, and we are swept into the afterglow of the sun.

18
Flying

Two minutes ago, the kitty cat from the fifth floor leaped out of the window.

A shriek lodged like a fish bone in my throat but never reached the air. Everything around me remained silent. Mouth agape, I stood rooted to the spot, only my eyeballs moving to follow the cat's flight path. Those few seconds might have lasted years.

Into my brain flashed various images, each more gruesome than the last. My hairs stood on end. What my eyes had seen, my brain extrapolated—several outcomes for each scenario. What would the actual ending be? How would all these moments combine to form a single event? I had no way of knowing, nor did I want to imagine.

I opened my eyes as wide as possible just as the large cat soared overhead, limbs outstretched, as if invisible webbing had sprouted between its front and rear legs so that it might be able to glide smoothly down on the air currents if it kept its limbs rigid. There actually is a thin membrane between cat claws like duck webbing, and the whole time it forced its toes apart, trying to catch the wind.

Observing this scene, I decided without question that cats were flying creatures, and this one would be able to touch down, not stopping unless it wanted to; if it never stopped, the outcomes in my brain would never transpire. I wanted it to plunge like this forever, a perpetual motion machine, never slowing.

For just this moment, I felt the ease and lightness of this form of flying and no longer needed to know how we'd ended up here, or why the cat had decided to exit through the window rather than taking the stairs or elevator.

Enchanted, I stared at the cat, stretching out those few seconds, which dilated so much that the cat stopped falling. As for where it soared off to, when it would finally descend, I wasn't concerned. The only thing I cared about was that the cat was flying.

In reality, the cat swiftly became a free-falling object with a terminal velocity, and the arc of its trajectory described a perfect parabola. Even so, I couldn't stop myself from shutting my eyes the instant the cat hit the ground. Surely the image would completely shatter at this moment.

Then I slowly opened my eyes and found the image still intact—and the cat unharmed. There was a glimmer of terror in its eyes, but that too quickly dissipated. Surveying its new surroundings, it located an exit and scampered out of sight.

Flying had protected the cat, I thought, but I couldn't be sure. I looked down at my watch. Five minutes to eight—I'd woken earlier than usual, but there was no way I could get back to sleep, so I decided to go for a walk. The vegetable market closest to the flat should be open by now, I thought, but I couldn't be sure of that either.

Returning to my building with a bag of groceries, I heard my neighbors discussing what happened that morning, describing what they'd witnessed: how a cat flew past their windows, like a miracle. The story took a turn and landed upon a barrage of blame for the cat owner. My groceries and I followed everyone into the elevator. I filtered out their criticisms of the human and caught hold of every mention of the soaring cat until I was able to piece together in my brain the cat's entire arc. Standing in the elevator as it began to rise, I felt myself take off too.

19
Cat Ears

On any given day, a cat's ears will swivel 180 degrees in one direction, then 180 degrees the opposite way. A full circle or even more, n full circles. They hear everything in a complete round too. As a result, various sounds encircle cats. No matter where they go, those sounds seem to have hands and feet, which grab on to the fine hairs sprouting from their ears. That's why cats get startled by the slightest noise.

Cats hear things that humans can't. Their ears turn this way and that, like a couple of little satellite dishes picking up signals from all directions. Without a single warning sign, they suddenly grow alert, every joint in their bodies tensing, especially in their necks, where it seems as if a few hundred mechanical parts have all been activated at once. Cat ears transmit the sounds they pick up throughout the entire body, triggering mechanisms from reflexes to dilated pupils.

Cat's sensitivity to sound creates many opportunities for him to fritter away his time. He spends his days chasing after noises beyond human hearing, a great game for him. All alone in the flat, he sprints back and forth, tiring himself out so that he can barely catch his breath. But what is he actually after? Who is he playing with? There is no one to be seen. Are these mysterious uninvited guests his friends or enemies? Who even are they? I'm so curious about what these beings must look like and how they're able to absorb so much of Cat's attention, making him so pugnacious yet clownlike.

I've carried out secret investigations but didn't turn up a single clue. The only evidence that these visitors even exist is that Cat will be sitting there, perfectly fine, then in an instant his demeanor changes completely. With baffling abruptness, he startles and twitches. As if peril has abruptly descended. Cat chases after something, trying to corner them, and they pursue him in return, similarly penning him in.

Cat's ears are connected. Whenever I tell him to stop running and just be still for a moment, the words enter his left ear only to go straight through to his right, where they seep out, never to be seen again. Cat has never listened to a word I have to say, let alone taken one to heart. He scampers around the flat wildly no matter what I tell him. All I can do is comfort myself with the knowledge that he doesn't understand my language.

Each of Cat's ears contains a doorlike contraption that allows him to store all the noises he enjoys: opening a tin can, flushing the toilet, opening our door, and so on. Any of these sounds will bring him bounding happily over, lulling him into another spate of ecstasy. Cat files away all the noises he likes, a system of recordkeeping that makes sense only to him.

The wind is particularly beloved by Cat because it blows all kinds of sounds his way, some of which he enjoys; others he permits the wind to waft away again. A sort of regular flea market with treasures for him to rummage through. Cat is a picky customer, and he doesn't always find a noise to his liking. Nonetheless, playful as he is, he always looks forward to the wind's arrival.

On occasion, Cat will unpack the audio library in his

ears and sample it for the wind, which spins in a circle, to say it has brought similar sounds this time too. Hearing this, Cat runs with the wind. The wind is faster, of course, and Cat has to sprint to keep up. It stashes Cat's favorite sounds atop cans, on the toilet, in doorframes, and whenever Cat comes upon one he likes, he jumps and grabs hold of it, full of gratitude for the wind.

Cat's joy spreads from his inner to outer ears, from where it can be passed on to the wind. Infected with this pleasure, the wind ferries it farther afield. Before it can get far, other winds will have tugged this happiness apart, dispersing it in all directions.

This arrangement suits Cat. One wind is much like another, just as it's hard to tell between one joy and another. It's all happiness.

20
Cat-and-Seek

Someone once asked me if Cat ever gets bored, and I had to admit that I hadn't the slightest clue—I'd never noticed. Since then, I've started paying more attention to Cat's daily routine, only to find that he spends virtually all his time asleep.

Many times, I've seen Cat walk from one end of the living room to the other, a journey of maybe a dozen yards. Even so, he stops several times along the way to rest, eyelids drooping the entire while, looking unbearably tired. If I don't call his name, he might fall asleep right there and then.

I don't know why cats are so drowsy. I've read that the average feline spends seven-tenths of its life asleep, which frankly I envy. As far as I'm concerned, being able to sleep as much as you want is pure heaven! I suffer from insomnia and spend many nights flipping over in bed like a pork bun on a griddle. Cats, though, can fall asleep in a single second. If Cat could donate some of his slumber to me, so he could sleep a little less and I a little more, wouldn't that be just right?

While Cat dozes, I like poking him with a finger so he cracks open one eye, realizes it's only me, contentedly shuts it again, and rolls over to fall back asleep. If I poke him again, he responds in exactly the same manner, completely disregarding me. So I go poke, poke, poke, not letting up until he finally wakes up for real, at which point he has no choice but to stand, arch his back into a stretch, then slowly stroll away, still ignoring my existence.

In order to evade my teasing. Cat keeps finding new sleeping spots. It takes me a while to find each one. The more he hides himself, the more I want to uncover him. We're playing a game of cat-and-seek.

Cat conceals himself in tiny spaces, curled into a ball, eyes shut, having a brief snooze or a proper sleep. He never lets out a single sound, the better to stay hidden. Drawers, wardrobes, under the bed, behind a door—all places he might be. Once Cat is out of sight, he won't show himself until he gets hungry or hears a disturbance. He can stay hidden an entire day with no issue. Then again, as long as I'm home, how could he hope to stay hidden so long? I certainly wouldn't be able to let him out of my sight for that many hours. After a short while, I'd go in search of him. If I don't see him right away, I start to get anxious, unable to settle, and begin buzzing around the house like a headless fly, seeking Cat everywhere.

In the end, I'm the one who has nothing better to do, not Cat.

When I can't find Cat, I long for his presence all the more eagerly. The worst thing is when I desperately need some catness, and he's nowhere to be found. Each new hiding place gets abandoned as soon as a human discovers it, and he'll move on to the next one.

There are times when Cat hides himself too well—so not only can I not find him but he's lost to himself too. There have been a few times when Cat has only emerged very late at night, so hungry that the light has gone out of his eyes. When he sees his food, he dashes over and begins wolfing it down. On these occasions, I feel he must have gotten lost in his new hiding place and only found his way back with a lot of effort.

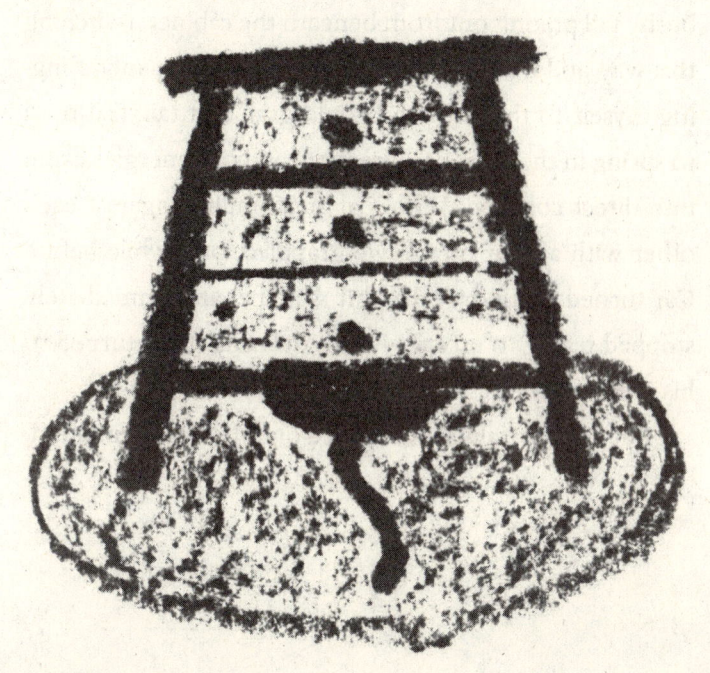

I once helped Cat search for himself but only exhausted myself to no avail. Finally, I slumped on the couch, and as my eyes swept over the TV stand, I happened to see a bushy tail poking out from beneath the cabinet, twitching this way and that. Reflexively, I sprang off the sofa, flinging myself to the floor so I could grab that tail. Cat tried to spring in the opposite direction, and our energies came into direct collision. With Cat and I pulling against each other with all our might, we grappled for a while before Cat turned around, realized it was me, and immediately stopped trying to escape. Finally relaxing, he returned to his previous softness.

Cat and I are always delighted once he has been found.

21
A Catlike Woman

I once heard Husband remark, "My wife is a catlike woman."

This was a lovely thing to hear, and a secret joy blossomed in my heart. I imagined him elaborating, "She's just like a cat: independent, elegant, beguiling." Yet despite my attentive ear, I somehow failed to hear him say those words—in fact, he fell completely silent. As if he'd never spoken the first sentence, so naturally the words didn't follow.

It's okay, I told myself. I just needed to be patient. After all, we lived together, we had all the time in the world. I didn't ask him about it because I was so confident that the explanation would arrive unbidden. I waited and waited, my expectations not lessening one little bit. In fact, they grew stronger until I began imagining myself into a cat with the same enchanting personality that all cats exhibit. Some people use "catlike" to mean a human who isn't easy to understand or control. A catlike woman must surely be full of allure, not in a superficial way but in one that emanates a strong attraction from deep within, making everyone want to get closer to her while also maintaining a respectful distance.

Women are the most catlike creatures on the planet. As a catlike person myself, I decided I ought to have enough tenderness and patience to wait for an explanation. I wouldn't be anxious; I would simply wait. A very long time passed. Husband didn't give away the faintest hint of what might have followed that fragment of conversation, as if he'd forgotten he ever uttered it. My forbearance began to fray, wearing thin my cat-resemblance.

Sometime after that, I distinctly sensed a cat whooshing out of my body and disappearing into the ether. I had utterly lost my catness. Now I found myself thinking nonsense all day long, turning circles in my brain. What could Husband's behavior mean? Why had he foregone the second half of that sentence?

Now I was no longer catlike, I grew short-tempered, quick to anger. As soon as the fuse was lit, I would tense up, losing all my self-confidence. Looking in the mirror, I could scarcely believe this was me. Obviously there was a likeness, but I didn't want to look like that.

More days slip by. Since the catness left my body, I had grown scrawny. Then the day came when, out of the blue, Husband stood next to me and said, "My wife is a catlike woman." With that, he began shaving, his face covered in thick foam so I couldn't make out his expression in the mirror. If he'd never brought up those words again, I could have left them to fester in my heart, pretending he'd never spoken them. Time would have worn them away. But now he'd repeated the same infuriating half-baked thought. Fury roared uncontrollably through my lungs, and I choked out the words, "Could you please kindly explain how I'm like a cat?"

I wasn't enraged because he'd once again left me dangling but rather because I no longer felt anything like a cat. Startled by my fierceness, Husband gaped. The flames kept blazing in my chest, roaring even higher, and my voice got even louder: "Don't call me a cat. I'm no longer a cat."

He looked puzzled and pointed to the floor. "All I mean is you leave strands of hair everywhere, just like Cat does. All this fluff belongs to you and Cat." He gestured in the mirror at his own crew cut.

I reeled and felt my face grow scalding hot. Awkwardly hanging my head, I smiled to myself, not saying a word. In that moment, I felt the catness return to my body.

22
Black Cloud

Friends left their little black cat with us for a week. Every inch of this kitty from head to toe was completely black. Her fur and skin gleamed darkly. Even her claws and nose were like pitch.

The little black cat patrolled our flat, swaggering. She had to map out her new territory, never mind that it already contained a cat. She moved with the boldness of one who'd seen something of the world and already met others of her species. Meanwhile, Cat had never seen any other cats. He'd always assumed that, apart from himself, the world contained nothing but humans, or perhaps he thought he was human too and never regarded himself as a cat in the first place.

The first time Cat saw this other cat, shock and confusion were written all over his face. He couldn't believe there existed another living thing so close in appearance. After he'd verified that this was actually happening, the atmosphere grew tense. Both creatures began letting out hissing sounds, a warning of impending danger.

All of a sudden, Cat developed a strong territorial sense. He wouldn't allow another cat to pass through his turf. If she advanced an inch, so would he, following her every step of the way, looking for an opening to launch his attack on this uninvited guest and to chase her off. His attention was laserlike; his eyes never left her. His gaze was utterly focused on her body, as if he wished he could set it alight.

The pair of them kept up this stalemate all day long. The little black cat tried to hide but couldn't resist her curiosity when it came to these new surroundings. In the face of this great enemy, Cat didn't let up for half a second. They advanced and retreated, feinted and parried, but never started fighting for real.

At night, when drowsiness arrived, I left both cats in the living room while I went off to the bedroom, shut the door, and fell asleep.

In the middle of the night, a yowling arose from the living room. The kitties were dementedly chasing each other, knocking over anything in their path, an endless series of skirmishes and clangs. I glanced at the time: past three o'clock.

Lying in bed, I hesitated about whether to involve myself. I listened a while longer, but there was no sign of a truce, so I dragged myself to the living room. I stood in the center of the room, but they completely ignored me and continued baring their teeth at each other. Other than the faint gleam of her eyes, a pair of green beans, nothing of the little black cat could be seen. Where were her belly, her limbs, her tail? They were invisible in the darkness, having transformed into shapelessness, a sort of inky gas. All I could see was Cat chasing after a little sooty cloud, lunging at it only to come up empty.

The little black cat's visit was like a storm cloud drifting into the sky above my flat. Lightning streaked from the space between the two cats, followed by thunder and heavy rain, *pitter patter pitter patter*. . . . The summer rains had arrived early and were in my flat.

For several nights after that, I found myself automatically waking in the middle of the night and getting up to check on the cats. Finally, walking from the bedroom to the living room, I almost tripped over something—an object that jumped and shrieked at the same time I did. Kitten had decided to sleep right in my path, but her entire body had melded with night into a single entity.

After several days of quarreling and fierce battle, the cats were bone-weary. Nighttime gradually grew quiet. On this night, Cat fell asleep leaning against the softest imaginable surface. When he woke the next day, he realized he'd been pillowing his head on the little black cat's belly all night long.

23
Springing Cat

Occasionally, Cat is liquid, formless, flowing in all directions, able to slip through cracks much smaller than his body. Most of the time, he manages to configure himself into the shape of a cat. What is his actual form? We might never know. I've never met anyone who's concerned about this phenomenon—most people only care about having a cat that conforms to the shape they expect. A cat's true form isn't important to them.

I keep discovering new cat shapes. There are so many of them, and they are so unstable, that even if I were to set out to record them, I wouldn't necessarily capture every one. Luckily my task is just to mind Cat, not to research him, so it doesn't matter if I miss some of his variations.

When I do see him take on a structure I haven't encountered before, I take the opportunity to witness this wondrous sight.

Not long ago, for instance, I learned that Cat is a spring.

I'd bought a new printer, and Husband helped me install it, spending ages poring over the instructions. Finally, we heard a beep, which confirmed that the printer was connected. Impatiently, I slid a stack of white paper into its tray and watched as each sheet was sucked into the machine, emerging covered densely in black words.

As the printer worked, its *whirr whirr whirr* attracted Cat, who had never seen a printer in his life. This rigid, squarish fellow intrigued him. He ambled over, thought about sniffing at it, but then cautiously circled behind me instead from where he could safely observe this newly arrived monster and determine if it was safe.

The second document began printing, *whirr whirr whirr*, and Cat took a step forward, peering closely, only to take fright and retreat several feet back.

He didn't dare approach again, but crouched where he was with panic all over his face.

I wanted to help Cat understand that there was nothing to be scared of, no need to hide. I picked up a few of

the printed pages and brought them over to him, hoping he'd sniff at them and see that they weren't frightening at all. Instead, my simple action inadvertently pushed one of Cat's buttons.

In an instant, Cat leaped half a meter into the air, all four limbs leaving the ground at the same time, like a spring suddenly released from pressure, reaching such a height at such a speed that I could only marvel at it. Coming back to earth, as soon as his paws were firmly on the floor, he scrabbled backward an even greater distance. I hastily reached out to pet and soothe him, but that only made him recoil farther back. At this point, I could no longer hold back the laughter welling up inside me.

It's rare to catch sight of a cat-spring in action, and I'd never witnessed Cat losing his cool to this extent, boinging so high and so far. I formed the mental image of a springing cat: externally resembling a cat but actually composed of coil after coil encased in flesh.

Now, when I see Cat sitting quietly in one place, I believe he's storing up potential energy, charging the spring like a battery, so it's ready for use when he needs it.

Cat-springs are a rare sight, and you don't feel their coils when petting them. Only when a cat gets a fright does this power activate, thrusting itself out of peril. Every cat's body has a hidden button, a long-buried secret that transforms it from cat to cat-spring. No one knows where this button is located except for the cats themselves. Cats may normally seem soft and malleable, capable of being kneaded into all kinds of shapes—who could have imagined they would contain such a mechanism as well?

24
Mirror

Husband bought a rectangular mirror to lean against our bedroom wall.

Cat walked past once, twice, thrice . . . without noticing it. Then, finally, he happened to stroll directly toward the mirror—and was astonished to see another cat walking toward him. He froze, staring straight at the intruder with just as much curiosity and enmity as his first encounter with the little black cat.

The cat in the mirror glared back at him with the same intensity—a warning. Cat took a few paces back, and so did Other Cat. Cat arched his back, and so did Other Cat. Sensing something was amiss, Cat's fur stood on end in a show of aggression, but Other Cat responded in kind at the very same moment. Flustered now, Cat went swiftly into full battle stance. Steeling himself, he sprinted at his opponent and pounced, claws at the ready, taking a hefty swipe—only to smack the glass with a resounding *thunk*, claws skittering helplessly across the smooth surface.

Cat hit the ground and looked left and right, as did Other Cat. Resuming the attack, Cat found himself somehow unable to lay a paw on the enemy. He scrabbled wildly at the mirror, the two of them clawing *ping pang* at the glass.

Cat suddenly stopped, retracted his claws, and fixed his eyes on the mirror. The two cats glared at each other, then something suddenly softened, and their gazes turned tender. Cat tilted his head to one side, and so did Other Cat. Cat batted his eyes, and Other Cat reciprocated. Cat looked all around, then back at the mirror. By this point, his demeanor had returned to its usual vague amiability. Drawing closer, he took a sniff at his counterpart but smelled nothing. Relaxing his vigilance, he moved another step closer and stretched his head forward, hoping to rub against Other Cat's neck. Other Cat leaned toward him too, and they spent a while nuzzling each other, eyes shut in ecstasy.

Finally, Cat slowly opened his eyes. It was dawning on him that something still wasn't quite right. Straightening up, he began scrutinizing his surroundings again. Eventually it hit him: no matter what he did, Other Cat would do the same, but opposite. The same rhythm, speed, distance.

Cat let out a confused cry. Other Cat's mouth opened too.

Refusing to give up, Cat pressed his nose against the mirror again. He would sniff his way to the truth. His snout went forward and back, thoroughly investigating every inch of not just the mirror but its surroundings too. Not one whiff of another cat, just his own cat self.

He stood stock-still, waiting for the miracle of his imagining to take place. Other Cat waited too. Time passed. Cat's body grew limp. His legs splayed as he succumbed to sleep on the floor, showing his belly, licking drowsily at his chest fur.

Since then, Cat has taken to gazing at his reflection several times a day. The hostility in his eyes is long gone, replaced by something harder to pin down. He sits there for a long time, growing fonder and fonder of what he sees.

After some time, Husband moved the mirror to another room. Cat didn't find its new location right away and instead looked in horror at the empty wall, snuffling and pawing at it before stalking away. He returned after a while only to find the wall still blank.

It took Cat an entire day to track down the mirror. Once again, he crouched before it, staring unblinkingly at Other Cat, sunk in a world of his own.

25
Cat Fluff

Remember when my husband said women shed everywhere, just like cats?

I disagree—cat fur and women's hair are two completely different things. Don't be misled into thinking just because they look similar and fall every day that there exists any true likeness between them. From beginning to end, human hair is dead. As soon as it lands on the floor, it loses the vitality it once had. Any hair not on a living scalp is a corpse. Cat fur, on the other hand, becomes something entirely new once it leaves the cat's body.

We don't measure cat fur by individual strands but in units of clumps. Even tangled together, these hairs are so light, so silky, that they can still tumble through the whole flat. Every single day, cats naturally shed their fur and it floats in the air, light as the fluff from a willow tree.

While only some willow and poplar trees produce cat-kins, every single kitty that grows fur also sprouts cat fluff. Strictly speaking, these cat-kins are a natural phenomenon, not manufactured. In spring and autumn, cat-kins come particularly thick and fast, drifting around as if they carry cat seeds and must travel to be propagated farther afield.

Cat-kins look beautiful as they skim through the air. They stay aloft for quite some time, then tire and settle down, or simply come to earth when the air currents have stalled. Sometimes they carelessly allow dust to hitch a ride until too many motes pile on and their combined weight sinks the fur.

Seeing the floor covered in cat-kins, Husband carts out the vacuum cleaner to capture them. Most are unable to evade his pursuit, but a few lucky specimens survive to land up in other parts of the flat.

The cat-kins on the floor go unrecognized by Cat. He pays them no attention or else mistakes them for food and tries to eat them. At no point does he seem to understand that they originally came from his own body. And when

they knit together into a furball, Cat might get excited enough to bat one around, though even then it's no more than a toy to him.

Cat produces cat-kins constantly, and the instant one is sent into the world, it loses any memories of its origins. And so amnesiac, desultory cat-kins can only float around at random but will never be able to return to the cat from whence they came.

Most unlucky of all are the cat-kins who get sucked up by the vacuum cleaner right away, their life span no more than a few minutes.

Every cat-kin has a different fate. If they're lucky, they're able to pick their moment and struggle free just as the cat passes an open window, escaping into the expanse of the outside world. The next best way out is to cling on to a human's clothing to be smuggled outdoors whenever that person next leaves the building.

My own clothes are frequently covered in cat-kins, which hang on stubbornly no matter how I try to get rid of them. These little tagalongs broadcast a very particular message, no matter the time or season: *hey, everyone, I have a cat*. This tends to lead to interesting conversations. Cat-kins don't annoy me at all—in fact, they make other people like me more, and we inevitably end up chatting happily about cats, because cat lovers deeply appreciate one another. Sometimes I'll be out when I spot someone else bearing their own cat-kins, and we exchange a knowing smile. As we hang out, the cat-kins detach themselves from our bodies and exchange hosts, so I end up bringing someone else's cat-kins home, while they've done the same to mine. And just like that, these swatches of cat fur have successfully gotten us to transplant them.

26
Tail-Chasing

Behind every cat is something he doesn't quite understand: his tail.

The tail sprouts fuzzily from the bum. As kittens grow up, their tails become longer and thicker—but they don't seem to realize they're becoming adults and certainly don't know they have great big tails attached to them. Rather, they vaguely sense there is something following them, but when they turn around, their tails droop and they see nothing.

After many failed attempts at finding out what lurks behind them, cats give up and slowly get used to the sensation of being tailed at all times.

It's not like cats are constantly turning around to seek

their tails. They might look back once in a while, but their tails assume this is part of a game and swiftly duck out of sight. As time goes on, it begins to seem as if tails have a life of their own, and although they happen to be conjoined, cats are cats and tails are tails.

Cats generally don't seem to believe they have tails, while tails don't regard themselves as belonging to cats.

As a result, cat tails often seem outside of their body's control, moving according to rhythms of their own. Even when Cat has been snoring for ages, his tail continues unabated, unfurling and snapping back as if it contains a length of elastic and is playing a game with itself. Cat is never woken by these shenanigans, so sound are his slumbers. The ponderous swaying of his tail has a hypnotic effect on him. Swing to the left, then to the right. *Tick tock tick tock . . .* drowsiness follows.

One time, Cat had raised a rear leg during a meticulous grooming session and was licking away at his hindquarters when, all of a sudden, his head froze in midair, eyes round and staring. A large, hairy object had hovered into his view, just below his own tailbone. Stunned, Cat stared fixedly, his concentration slackening. No one could have known what he was thinking. After a very long time, he seemed to come back to earth but continued facing this unfamiliar object with utter astonishment all over his face. Meanwhile, the tail was out of control, moving to a rhythm all of its own, now side to side, now up and down, smugly tormenting Cat.

With a sharp movement, one of Cat's front paws darted out to grab hold of the tail, bringing it to his mouth, while a rear leg tried but failed to stomp on it. Regardless, Cat continued gnawing, now and then sticking out his tongue to lick it too.

The tail struggled for a moment in Cat's paw before

slithering out like a snake. All four paws now on the ground, Cat chased off in its direction, jaws wide open in an attempt to clamp down once more on the furry interloper. He could see the very tip of the tail, close enough that he could reach it if he stretched his head just a little forward. Yet how peculiar—each movement ahead was met with a retreat. No matter how far his head extended, the tail shrunk back just as much. Trying to reach it, Cat moved faster, but the tail sped up too, in an accelerating game of catch. Finally, Cat and the tail were spinning in a circle on the ground. The tail's velocity as it fled lent momentum to Cat, while his pursuing energy likewise fueled its flight. Two sources of kinetic energy endlessly replenishing each other, creating a perpetual motion machine. They're still going at it to this day, unable to stop.

27
Plant Assassin

Husband likes to say there are two plant assassins in our family: me and Cat.

Before Cat, few plants in our household were able to escape my demonic clutches. Whenever Husband went on a work trip, they'd be left begging for water. Some didn't manage to cling on till his return and wilted away from this earth. Each time, sorrow-stricken Husband would berate me. Feeling wronged, I'd retort, "But I didn't do anything to them!"

"That's the point," he'd snap, furious. "It's because you didn't do anything that they died."

In the end, Husband started cultivating only extremely hardy plants, which I was forbidden to interfere with.

Neither of us could have foreseen that, once rescued from me, his beloved houseplants would fall victim to the slaughter of Cat. As soon as he arrived in our home, Cat began a reign of terror that immediately vaulted him past me to number one in the plant-killer charts. I rejoiced that the resultant carnage had, for once, nothing to do with me.

At the end of his rope, Husband held Cat up at arm's length and gave him a good scolding. Cat merely stared limpidly back with his round, clear eyes, utterly innocent and hapless. Finally, Husband realized the futility of his disapproval and set him back down. Even then, Cat knew how to use his own cuteness to exonerate himself, and he truly saved me too. If not for his presence, the few surviving houseplants would surely have succumbed to my ministrations.

As far as Cat is concerned, plants aren't for admiring or sniffing at but for sleeping on. Whenever the weather is nice and Cat is in a good mood, he climbs atop a houseplant and snoozes amid its vegetation, rolling his plump body this way and that, allowing the sunlight to baste every cranny. Beneath his weight, the leaves and branches crunch and rustle, speaking their final words. Cat ignores them, dozing contentedly all afternoon. By the time he wakes up, so much of the plant will be mulched into the soil that there's no way it could spring back to its original shape.

There are also times when Cat grabs hold of a peculiar inspiration (who knows where from) and declares a particular plant his sworn enemy. Lunging at it, he'll wrestle and bite in a display of overstimulated vigor. After a few rounds of this, the plant will be decimated, and Cat swaggers off the battlefield every inch the victor, leaving in his wake a chaotic scene of strewn leaves and branches. Without a word, Husband sweeps away the corpses of his fallen soldiers and disposes of them. He has trained himself not to betray any emotion in these moments, having psychologically prepared himself for the arrival of this day.

After a plant's passing, the soil that once housed it gradually grows hard and dry. Cat continues treating it as a bed, sprawling atop its surface and snoozing away, limbs splayed, photosynthesizing in the stead of the eradicated plant. With each absorption of sunlight, Cat's fur manufactures particles of joy, bringing sheer happiness to Cat when licked up and to humans when inhaled, so much so that we forget all about the plants he murdered, and even Cat no longer remembers that he is a killer.

28
Scene Partners

Cheep cheep, the birds raucously chirp outside our windows. Cat comes running at the sound, showing enormous enthusiasm and curiosity. His jowls will not stop quivering, his eyes sparkle, and he wants nothing more than to lunge at our feathered friends. Unfortunately for him, they are in the sky, out of reach but in sight. He can only stare in frustration, his claws skittering on the glass.

And still the birds cry out, fluttering back and forth in the open air. Two or three one way, a lone bird the other. On the sill, Cat isn't still for a single moment but leaps this way and that too. His body twists to keep up with their flight paths, his head swaying this way and that, like a metronome. The birds don't so much as glance at Cat; his excitement is entirely unreciprocated.

There are times when the windowsill becomes a stage with a beam of sun in place of a spotlight, illuminating Cat so every strand of fur boasts a radiant sparkle, a cloud of light encircling him brilliantly. Cat seems to be wearing a rhinestone-studded outfit, a shimmering layer every bit as dazzling as the most famous star.

The sounds emerging from Cat's lips at these times are no longer meows but chirps, and the corners of his mouth twitch as his regular speech is tempered into song. His body gyrates without his realizing it, echoing the flap of bird wings, trying to incorporate everything about them into himself.

And still the birds soar past again and again, *cheep cheep*, ignoring Cat's blandishments.

Cat is fully consumed by his performance, demonstrating all kinds of skills. Now he crouches with a fixed stare, now he flings himself at the glass, now he claws at the firmament, trying by any means to get closer to the birds or at least to earn their approval. He also hopes that by flapping his paws in this way, they'll somehow sprout into wings and allow him to ascend so he can frolic with the birds on high. Spotted from a distance, Cat looks like he's attempting a rather beautiful jig.

Cat will never get his paws on a bird, but that doesn't stop him from trying. He is intelligent enough that it's entirely within the realm of possibility that he's already worked out the distance between himself and the birds, measured with his quivering whiskers. He might understand it's an impossible task, which has become the basis of this performance, but has become so committed to his role that he is unable to extricate himself, and so must continue till he's expended every last bit of energy in his body. Only then can he find peace.

By the time he achieves this, the birds will have flown away. Fully spent, Cat slumps limply, recalling the performance he's just enacted, a solo show with the birds for unwitting scene partners.

The curtain slowly falls. Having become part of Cat's theater, even the birds' departure is an aesthetic marvel.

A flock of gray-brown birds limned by the setting sun, their wings ferrying glimmers of light that slowly melt into their feathers, transfiguring them into flying beings of gold. They swoop farther and farther away, finally disappearing into a crimson cloud.

29
Many Moons

There is one moon in our sky, which we call "the moon." A satellite of Earth, it spins while orbiting our planet. Its surface is covered in ranges of hills and studied through a telescope; it is pitted with craters of all sizes. These depressions gobble up some of the sun's rays, allowing the rest to be reflected back to us as the soft radiance of moonlight.

Virtually everyone loves the moon. We adore its purity, clearness, elegance, and imperfect roundness. There are many tales of the moon, from which it's clear that human imagination is drawn to closing the gap between ourselves and the moon. After all, there is only one moon, and no one can hope to possess it alone.

To be honest, one moon isn't enough for us. We don't

even get to see it hanging above us every night. And when it is there, imagine dividing it up between the entire human race: carve it into several billion pieces, and each person's share would be reduced to a chunk of ordinary rock, dull and unchanging.

It was only when I started living with Cat that I realized: we may only have one moon in the sky, but there are others scattered here on Earth. All over our floor, Cat sheds his claw casings at regular intervals, perfect little translucent crescents, so many I have lost count.

When I press my fingertip to one of them, it sticks and I feel like I'm holding the tiniest moon in the whole world.

These crescents are exquisite and pearlescent, cropping up wherever Cat has been, gleaming from every corner of the flat.

Sometimes I find moons wedged into sofa crevices, reclining on my desk, shimmering on the quilt. Trace Cat's footsteps and you're sure to stumble upon an adorable arc. I pick up these cat-moons and place them in my palm, where they sit, no larger than a grain of rice, the littlest possible moon suspended in the littlest possible sky.

These days, I no longer need to wait for nightfall or astronomical events to admire the moon. At any hour, even

broad daylight, I can see and touch the moon. Cats grant us wishes without even trying, just as a willow branch carelessly thrust into the ground will flourish. All in all, cats play their part as moon-movers, parceling the big moon into countless miniatures, each of them perfectly formed in an archetypal crescent.

Get a cat, and you'll gain many moons. Wherever cats go, moons follow, and wherever one finds moons, one will invariably find people.

As the moons add up, I sometimes wonder: How different are they from stars? The defining characteristic used to be that there was only one moon but many stars, right? But then I look up at the night sky and notice the solitary moon and remember that this one still stands solo. There hasn't been any multiplying up there.

What *has* increased is my attraction to the moon, and my reliance on Cat. No matter what, I have faith that Cat will continue manufacturing many, many moons.

30
Unity

It used to be that Cat was Cat, and I was me. Then the day came when Cat and I became one.

It was a perfectly ordinary day. When I understood that Cat and I were now a single entity, it didn't strike me as at all shocking or strange. I didn't fight the reality, probably because my subconscious had begun considering this possibility long ago. Besides, nothing about our outward appearances had changed—Cat still looked like Cat, and I still looked like myself.

I seldom go out, and Cat leaves the flat even more rarely. An otaku and a house cat sharing a living space, together all day long. I'm often at my computer writing, and Cat comes over to nuzzle me. Or else he'll be asleep, and

I'll carry my laptop over to him. Naturally, with the passage of time, we've fused together.

When I realized that Cat and I had melded, my initial reaction was amusement. That day, I'd been writing an essay, while Cat dozed using my arm as a pillow. My hands *clack-clacked* away at the keyboard, not disturbing him in the slightest. Unruffled, he snoozed peacefully, showing no sign of irritation. I began moving my arms as vigorously as possible, but he merely peeked open his eyes, surveyed his surroundings, and shut them again. No matter what I did, he remained still, as if he were just another appendage, just as some scientists claim that smartphones have essentially become part of our bodies. People no longer put down their devices, eyes fixed to their screens whether they're eating or walking, even using these machines to lull themselves into sleep come bedtime. Now that we're inseparable from our phones, they've replaced some human functions, which has in turn eroded our abilities in certain areas—though the phone companies try to put a good spin on it by claiming that, actually, our lives have become more convenient.

By contrast, my fusion with Cat hasn't been dependency forming. I've even forgotten about the existence of my phone. With Cat around, I'm no longer distracted, and I don't need anything else. Cat sometimes grows out of my lap, or in the crook of my arm, or on my shoulder. More and more, we're no longer separable, a single body. When he's leaning against me, or when I have my fingers buried in his fur, it's hard to say whether my body has sprouted a cat or if he is the one who birthed me. In any case, he is in my eyes, my nose, my consciousness, and so I want to write Cat down so he can live in my words too.

When I do leave the apartment, even though Cat is no longer physically with me, he still grows in my heart. I think of him every single moment. My eyes unwittingly flick to wherever I think stray cats might be, seeking out others of his kind, hoping the cat-kins that cover my body will attract them.

It's not just me—Cat has undergone a metamorphosis too.

Gradually, Cat has lost his sense of catness and frequently thinks of himself as human. I'm not quite sure how he learned this, but when he wants to tell us what he's thinking or feeling, he now wheedles or complains in the exact tones of a human child. Often Husband and I will get startled by these cat-person cries, then we'll burst

out laughing. At mealtimes, Cat will often leap uninvited onto the table, as if we prepared a spread for him. One of us only has to call the other for dinner and Cat will appear, bringing his face close to each plate, giving each dish a good sniff, then crouching nearby waiting to be fed.

At night, Cat jumps up onto the bed to sleep alongside Husband and me. In the winter especially, he burrows beneath the blanket and snores away, pressed tightly against me. At these moments, Cat must feel especially human—he needs a bed, a warm quilt, and a loved one to lie next to.

31
Doppelgänger

Husband likes to joke that Cat is my real lover. He claims that my expression doesn't change when I see him, but I can't stop the corners of my mouth from turning upward whenever I catch sight of Cat. Husband doesn't mind—he's not the jealous type. He came to love Cat because of me, he says—loving Cat is just the same as loving me. Cat and I are sometimes fused into a single entity, but Cat also has the ability to be my doppelgänger.

As my doppelgänger, Cat is my other self. He loves running the household and meticulously manages the mundane day-to-day chores. All day long he patrols the flat, lying here or sitting there, taking an inventory of every item that we own, not forgetting the dust on it—he believes every mote that lands in the apartment belongs to us too. He takes careful stock of the dust each day, making sure the amount hasn't changed. Husband often complains that I'm unhygienic because I don't like cleaning. Frankly, I believe housework is a cruel habit, a way of erasing history. Like me, Cat is unwilling to wipe away all traces of himself from our lives.

Ever since becoming my doppelgänger, Cat has relied on eating dust to maintain his appearance. Luckily he's still my Cat. He looks the same, and there's still the same quantity of dust in the flat—there's no way he'd ever eat it all. With his rough tongue, he licks at the surface of a vase, taking a count of the dust motes on its surface. The more, the tastier. Too little dust leads to a blander flavor profile.

All Cat's toys—scratching posts, laser pointers, bells, stuffed mice, the bowl he eats out of—are blanketed in a thin film of dust, which makes it easy for him to find them. All these objects belong to Cat, and the dust is left each time he touches them. The thicker the layer, the more frequent his contact.

At night, when Cat wriggles under the covers, I get in there too and puff out a lungful of mesmerizing air. This causes Cat to melt so he can seep into my body. I

feel my temperature rise a few degrees. Like mercury, Cat rises from the soles of my feet to my chest, warming me thoroughly. When he can rise no more, he grows still and begins snoring, and I drop off too.

As we sleep, Cat continues appearing in my dreams. Bit by bit, I wipe clean the dream lens that reflects my subconscious. This way, I can see a little more of Cat in dreamland and remember these images more clearly when I wake.

In the mornings, I toss aside the covers, and Cat swiftly leaps out of my body. He floats in the air, and when the sun hits him, he is made of the same crystalline dust. Cat swirls around me, absorbing his fill of sunlight.

A new day. Cat coalesces once again into his usual form.

Cat drifts contentedly across the room, landing lightly wherever he fancies. Seek out the places that accumulate the most dust, and there you will find Cat.

32
Cat Virus

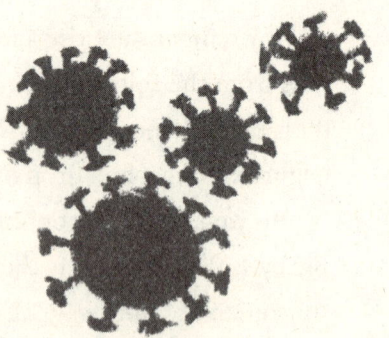

I went online one day and stumbled upon a news item about the Cat Virus currently exploding across the globe. Many humans have been infected, regardless of country, nationality, ethnicity. Cat Virus has spread far and wide, and the number of people getting sick is increasing.

I read up on the symptoms of many sufferers, who all reported low spirits, lack of energy, growing anxiety, emptiness, and despair. This sounded like some unheard-of illness, trafficked and disseminated by cats. Once infected, people became completely dependent on their felines, losing interest in humanity. Some were so severely afflicted that, after not receiving proper care in time, they passed away. Reading about their deaths, I pressed my hands to my bosom in terror. Just like that, I felt unable to breathe.

I cried out for Husband and, when he came, rubbed his chest and asked him, "Are you having any trouble breathing?" He shook his head. Maybe it was psychosomatic, but after reading that article, I began to feel myself coming down with the symptoms of Cat Virus.

A few days later, my friend Drizzle rang me up. She mentioned Cat Virus, asking if I'd heard about this new thing that was popping up all over the news. I said yes, I knew, and we began discussing it. Drizzle said she'd been experiencing more and more signs of the virus. Timorously, I confessed I was too.

After hanging up, I felt my heart fill with panic. Hurrying over to Husband, I told him I might have been infected. "Stop being a hypochondriac," he said, "and definitely don't go online to look up more diseases. In the end it won't be the germs that kill you; you'll die of fright scaring yourself with your self-diagnoses." I promised him I'd stop, but I couldn't help worrying about it, so when he wasn't looking, I went online and started scouring for more information. I needed to look up whether there was any treatment for Cat Virus.

I found a peculiar website whose interface was covered in terrifying headlines: "Warning Signs for Late-Stage Cat Virus," "Cat Virus Epidemic," and more. Cold sweat ran down my back. I kept scrolling, until I saw an ad for treating Cat Virus.

Curious, I clicked on it. The page displayed the account of a Cat Virus sufferer who'd been on his deathbed before discovering a miracle cure, which he now wished to share with the public for free. All you had to do, according to the website, was press your nose up against a cat's body and inhale deeply. Below this post were dozens of comments, every single one of them praising the effectiveness of this method. The only side effect was uncontrollable sneezing, and if you happened to have an allergy to fur, you might also find your face getting itchy and swollen.

Following a link on the page, I was redirected to a test consisting of thirty questions. Answering them confirmed I was at high risk of Cat Virus because my antibodies were weak. This was followed by a series of helpful tips for people in my demographic: If you don't have a cat, keep your distance. Don't allow them to come into your sight. Don't venture anywhere that cats prowl, and you'll remain uninfected. If you do have a cat, your only choice is to fight poison with poison and keep having cats for the rest of your life. Cats are both disease and cure, and abandoning cats will now cause you great physical and psychological harm. Not only that, you'll cause widespread damage within your community, because this illness doesn't just spread from cat to human but also between humans. Most of the people around you will end up as asymptomatic carriers or chronic sufferers.

This was both good and bad news. The bad news was that I was almost certainly infected with Cat Virus; the good news was that I could still be saved. As long as I continued living with Cat, the virus shouldn't affect me at all. Or at least, it would be slow acting, and I wouldn't end up dead. This suited me because I never intend to part with Cat.

33
Stretching

Cat opens and shuts one eye at a time, blinking away, readjusting to the light. His jaw stretches open into a yawn, revealing his sharp, narrow teeth. His drool is pulled into thin strands. His tongue licks the fur all around his lips.

There we go—my little guy's woken up. Right after regaining consciousness, Cat remains groggy, his eyes dull, his body sluggish. Often, he needs a proper stretch in order to dispel the remnants of his drowsiness.

Slowly rising to his feet, his body stiffens and a tremor shoots through it. His back arches into a bow, like a rounded bridge—his tail at one end, his head at the other. Tiny creatures like ants could easily clamber on and use him as a crossing; he'd be the perfect bridge for them. Af-

ter a while, Cat changes position. His front legs extend, while his bum presses to the ground, and he turns into a slide. Every bit of dust and loose fur rolls right off him.

I recall the slides I played on as a kid. These were often built in the shapes of animals, so from a distance, it would seem as if we were sliding down an elephant's trunk or along a giraffe's back. We were so happy, wandering among these enormous beasts.

Before my eyes, Cat slowly expands, gradually turning into a huge cat more than ten times his original size.

Now we are able to slide down Cat's back. We climb up his tail and stand on his rump—the highest point of

Cat. Then we slide down his spine, all the way to the back of his head. Inertia propels us over his scalp, and we go flying, a few stray strands of fur whooshing off with us. We are no different from these hairs, just as light and insignificant, hitching a ride on air currents to float around briefly before drifting back to earth.

Think about it: if each strand of cat hair is the same thickness as a human, how vast must Cat be in these moments! You can imagine how long a slide he makes. For all I know, the moon itself could roll down and tumble into the water, like the folktale of the monkeys retrieving the moon from the lake.

People claim the monkeys were deluded, that they were only ever reaching for a reflection, while the actual moon hung behind them the whole time. Regardless, when Cat stretches, his raised rump bumps up against the moon in the sky, which sometimes does get dislodged and slide down his back, and sometimes not. This is why there are some nights when we can see the moon overhead, and others when it is absent.

Cat only spends five seconds stretching, but five seconds in giant cat-time is a very, very long duration to us smaller creatures. Maybe five months, maybe five years.

His brief stretch creates a slide that, for us, is fixed in place, allowing us to play for a long time. We'll get tired of it before Cat has even finished stretching.

In front of us, Cat stretches. At the same instant, so does Giant Cat. He is ready. At any moment, people may go sliding down his back. I chuckle at the thought, and my brain fills with an image of this enormous cat with his raised rump.

34
Gift

A friend told me she knows someone who lives in the countryside and has a cat. This cat goes out to play every morning and always returns with a gift: a dead bird, a mouse corpse, a crushed cicada, a torn glove, a broken shoe, and so on. This poor individual doesn't know whether to laugh or cry or how to turn down these presents. Saying no wouldn't make a difference—the cat wouldn't understand, and the gifts would just keep coming.

I didn't really believe this story when I first heard it. Later, though, all kinds of strange objects began appearing in my bed. Recalling the story, I realized it was probably true.

I'm not sure when exactly Cat got into the habit of

leaving me presents. They're all different, and his reasons for giving them vary too.

Cat likes to deposit these items when I'm not looking. This way, by the time I discover them, it's too late—they're already there in front of me, and I can't refuse them. He brings me scrap paper, fruit peels, chewed-up toys, as well as his own pee and poop, all left on the covers while I'm sound asleep.

To start with, he dug paper and peels out of the trash can and bestowed them upon me. This probably began when he saw me tossing these items away, startling him. Sprinting over, he'd grab the wadded-up paper and bring it back to me. Like a dog, he'd beg for me to throw it again so he could retrieve it once more. After a few rounds of this game, it probably left enough of an impression on him that he wanted to keep playing.

As for the cat pee and poop, I used to think these were pranks he was playing on me. One night, I fell asleep earlier than usual and dreamed that Cat was taking a shit on me. Waking with a start, I realized I'd only been dreaming and let out a sigh of relief. When I lay back down, though, I smelled something awful and familiar. Rising up again, I shrieked. My dream was back, and this time it had infiltrated reality: there was a cat turd on the blanket, on my side of the bed. My cries jolted Husband awake. "What is it?" he said. "What's happened?"

I pointed at the poop. He ran outside for a look, then came jogging back in. "Aiyah, you shut the balcony door last night with the litter tray outside." I smacked my forehead. Of course, without access to his toilet, Cat had chosen me as an alternative.

Cat really is quite something. He's clever enough to know how to take revenge, and he has quite the temper. When he's unhappy, he can't be bothered to argue with you. Instead, he chooses this method of venting his dissatisfaction. These aren't gifts he's bringing me, but little bombs. I don't know what else to do except be very diligent in everything I do, so as not to anger him.

When he was six months old, Cat brought me a very special object. As always, he left it by my pillow while I was sleeping.

In the morning, I groped blearily for my phone, only to feel a small, sharp object poking into my palm. Bringing it closer, I saw a tiny milky-white tooth. Suddenly fully alert, I theorized where it had come from. It didn't look human, which left only one possibility: a cat tooth.

I shook Husband awake to tell him that Cat was losing his teeth.

Squinting, Husband carefully studied the tiny tooth I was holding between my thumb and forefinger, and confirmed that it was indeed a kitten tooth. I leaped out of bed, went in search of Cat, and pried open his mouth. Sure enough, a tooth was missing.

So this gift was also a milestone in Cat's life. According to human customs, when children begin losing their milk teeth, you have to drop the ones from the upper jaw behind a door, and toss the ones from the lower jaw up onto the roof. That's how you ensure that adult teeth will grow in properly.

I didn't do that, though. Instead, I hid the tooth away in a secret place—even Husband didn't know where it was. I wanted to see whether Cat would get a new tooth if his old tooth remained concealed. Call this a nasty little gift of my own—time for me to return the favor.

35
Foe

Cat runs wildly through the flat for no apparent reason. From south to north, west to east, completely out of control. As if a switch has been flicked, he moves like a machine at its fastest setting. As long as you enter the right information, Cat turns into a highly intelligent and unstoppable four-legged automaton, his route preprogrammed. He sprints through the house at breakneck speed without a hitch. Just when it looks as if he's about to crash into a wall, he easily swerves aside, his hind legs nimbly tapping the baseboard to send his body flying at a different angle, carving a graceful arc through the air, which is how he turns a corner and continues dashing in a different direction.

He runs and runs as if something is chasing him, leaving countless paw prints on the wall and even in the air as well. He goes up into the sky and comes back down to earth, always remaining alert, occasionally slowing down or even stopping altogether, head, ears, and eyeballs atwitch, studying his surroundings like a wuxia fighter from TV in the middle of a duel (two warriors, one standing in the dark, one in the light). His whiskers tremble as he seeks out his opponent. His front paws shoot out, his rear legs spring, and he's off again at speed.

His enemy seems able to fly too. Although it can't be seen, and I have no idea what it looks like, I can tell from Cat's expression that this is no ordinary foe. This enemy is able to move freely between reality and Cat's consciousness. Now into Cat's brain, now back into the room, driving Cat into a frenzy as he both tries to hunt down this creature and avoid becoming prey himself.

Cat and this uninvited guest are locked in an endless pantomime of chase. Every part of the flat is a battleground for them. The first time I saw Cat running like crazy, I was shocked and thought he might have something wrong with his brain—no matter how much I yelled at him, he ignored me. All I could do was be his audience, sitting on the couch and watching this senseless drama play out, waiting in suspense for the end.

Recounting this show later on, Husband and I both feel that Cat must have a foe hidden somewhere we couldn't see, or maybe not hidden at all but swirling all around us, invisible to humans but able to drive Cat into a tizzy.

Sometimes the smallest breeze will arrive, so faint it can barely be felt, only just ruffling my arm hairs but enough to send Cat into another round of battle with his great enemy. He'll lunge and crouch defensively, moving in such broad strokes that surely this would scare away any foe. When the wind finally stops, Cat quiets down. More often, there won't even be the slightest disturbance in the air and Cat will, nonetheless, with great resolve, enter the fray with his invisible foe.

36
Hollow Cat

Cat's belly bulges roundly, like those hydrogen balloons they sell outside the mall, the ones that float in midair: bulbous Mickey Mouses, Donald Ducks, SpongeBob SquarePantses, and so on. Cat swells too. Tie a thin string to him, and you loft him into the sky. As a prank, I could tug his tail to let out all the air, at which point he'd start coursing *whooooosh* through space, swooping crazily this way and that until he came back to earth as a feeble sack of skin. Deflated Cat would flop limply on the ground, immobilized, two dimensions instead of three, unable to stand or walk, no longer as proud and dashing as before. He'd stare at me with those pleading eyes, flashing an SOS. I often imagine this scenario and keep fleshing it out. It

always puts a wicked smile on my face. To think I could bring him that low!

After a while, I'd grab a handful of dry cat food and bring it to his mouth, let him gulp it down. That's not enough, so I follow it up with another until Cat's belly is full, and he's assumed his usual roundness. Having been inflated with cat food, Cat's belly is now cushioned with a thick layer of fat, which drags him downward, a burden of flesh he must carry around, afflicting him with the disease of laziness. Now he lounges on the floor, unmoving, belly sprawling like melting butter.

But no, Husband says that would be a waste of cat food. He comes up with a more economical method of reinflating Cat: simply blowing into him like a balloon. He already looks like one, after all, so why not treat him like one?

So I open my mouth wide and blow at Cat's tail. He begins swelling, expanding to the size of a ball. Now he is a hollow cat. He feels the same to the touch: the same smooth fur, the same taut belly, firm when I press on it, like an inflatable raft.

Weirdly, no matter how enormously round Cat gets, he can still easily squeeze into the narrowest spaces. Our bed is no more than four inches off the ground, and he can slide right in there—it's his favorite spot for an afternoon nap. He has a special technique: First, he pushes his head inside, leaving his rump in the air. Next, he farts, expelling all the extra air that would get in his way. This leaves him shriveled and flat as a board, so he can flop forward inch by inch. Before too long, his entire self is underneath the bed, nestled beneath the headboard.

There, he can doze in peace. In this confined space, no human is going to find or disturb him. If I want a glimpse of Cat at these moments, I have to press my whole body to the floor. As for playing with him, that has to wait till he wakes up of his own accord.

When he's finally had enough sleep and deigns to show himself, he emerges from beneath the bedside cabinet and stretches lazily. Taking a deep breath—no need for human inflation—he restores himself to his usual bulging self, the same size as before. While he's distracted, I tug at his tail and let the air back out. With a piercing shriek, he goes flying, zipping around till he's emptied out once more. Dragging his empty skin sac behind him, he collapses on the ground and looks at me again with those pleading eyes, waiting for me to replenish him once more.

37

Condensation

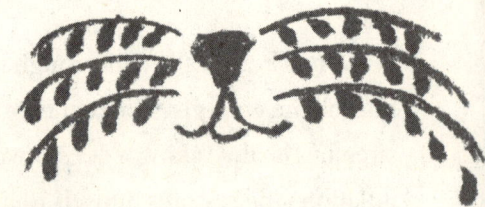

On evenings when the heat in the apartment grows oppressive, I feel as if a solid wedge of hot air presses down on my head. Unable to sit still, agitation building in my chest, I flap my collar and fan myself. "Quick, rain!" I exclaim. "Why can't it rain?"

Next to me, Cat is no longer still but circles me a few times. Then he sits back down, moistens a paw, and begins swiping at his face.

As the saying goes, when a cat washes his face, it's soon to rain.

The air grows humid and heavy before the storm. Thousands of water droplets can no longer sustain their own weight and need to find something to hang from or their heaviness will succumb to gravity, bringing them crashing down to earth, where they will vanish.

Clever water droplets come equipped with a pair of crystalline eyes, which are able to swiftly spot nearby objects that would make a good host. If they're lucky, they'll descend upon something absorbent: a blanket, clothing, any sort of fabric. When it threatens to rain, I rush to bring in the laundry—not because I think it's going to get soaked but so water vapor doesn't coalesce onto my clothes, making them damp and moldy, uncomfortable to wear. When a cotton blanket absorbs this moisture, it turns heavy and stiff, encasing the sleeper in a dank cave.

As a prophet of rain, Cat naturally attracts the attention of water droplets. You can imagine how his thick coat of fur is a living invitation to them. They swarm over and land on him so each strand harbors countless tiny water particles. Playing host to this much moisture, he can only walk with difficulty. Finally, unable to take another step, he sits down and starts lapping at his fur, his tongue scooping the water up into his stomach, lightening his load.

By licking up these molecules of water, Cat has consumed the vapor that would have become rain. Now his belly is full of natural rainwater, easing the storm a little.

Limpid drops of water dangle from Cat's whiskers: tiny, dazzling crystal grapes. Their weight pulls his whiskers into attractive arcs. Looking in the mirror, Cat is delighted to see their graceful curves and refuses to move away from his reflection, lost in self-admiration.

More and more moisture descends upon these bristles, pulling his whiskers down even farther. Cat's face stiffens, losing its mobility. His whiskers are no longer delicately curved but sadly drooping, losing all their dignity and beauty. Cat understands that he has now taken on too much water and is no longer good-looking. He shakes his head vigorously, then swipes at his whiskers with his paws.

In a moment, his whiskers are back to their normal bounciness, and his face is no longer weighed down. He gets rid of all the water particles, sending them back off into the air, allowing them to drift through the open window. Rising up, they quickly find a large cloud to take them in. Getting closer, they condense into an enormous, dark mass in the sky.

Not long after that, rain begins to fall.

38
Cat Mischief

Cats and cat mischief might resemble each other, but they're two completely different things. It's easy to mix them up if you're not paying attention, and some people even believe cat mischief is something sloughed off by cats. And sure, there may only be a fine line separating the two. Cat mischief is just a cat, plus numerous little playful pranks and plots, plus more nefarious things that have to be kept from the light of day. Remove these from the equation and you have a cat; add them back and you have cat mischief.

Cats have tremendously good eyesight, so even things that must be kept out of sight and hidden in deep places will be spotted by them in a trice. Cats know every bit of cat mischief and recognize all of them on sight. Cats are playful by nature and are filled with curiosity for all things, so even though they know cat mischief is naughty, they can't resist taking part or seeing what it feels like to be wayward.

To move between cat and cat mischief, or back again, is very easy. All a cat has to do is conceive of an evil thought or nasty trick, and it turns into cat mischief. Let go of these ideas, and it's a cat once more.

This is Cat's favorite game, moving between these two states. It's easy to play and doesn't take up too much energy, since a single thought is enough to effect the transformation. Most cats spend a portion of each day on this game of changeabout. The shift between the two is instantaneous, occupying the same space and time, leaving humans confused as to which is which.

If you see damp paw prints on the ground, you'll know cat mischief is afoot. Probably a cat has been playing with the water in the toilet bowl or basin, morphing it in an instant into cat mischief. As soon as cats see water, their playful hearts dive in like stones being flung into a lake, splashing up waves of sheer fun.

Cat mischief is crafty. Prints might give it away, but it can also cover its tracks, making it impossible to catch. Humans can't even be certain what it looks like.

Were I to follow these paw prints, they would lead me

out to the balcony, where I'd see Cat with his limbs stretched out, toasting his paws in the sunlight. I'd be a step behind, in other words, cat mischief having already reverted to cat. There is Cat, basking in the warmth of the sun, getting ready for a nap, his brain full of nothing but drowsiness—and of course, cat mischief is nowhere to be seen.

True cat mischief arrives out of nowhere and departs without a trace. I've never seen it myself, though I always seem to arrive just a second too late—it always eludes my grasp.

One time, I was working in my room, when I heard an ominous scraping in the living room. I hurried over and saw the cabinet door still swinging. I called out Cat's name and immediately the scraping stopped. When I went over, I saw the floor covered in scattered nuts. A short while later, Cat came ambling in from another room and strolled over to me as if nothing at all had happened. When I think of this now, I'm filled with regret. If only I hadn't shouted Cat's name! If I hadn't startled cat mischief away, maybe I would have caught sight of it.

Ever since then, Cat has been very cautious around me. Even when he does transform into cat mischief, I hardly ever notice.

158

39

Nine Lives in One

They say cats have nine lives, which makes it sound as if they have nine outfits so it doesn't matter if one of them tears—they still have eight more—no need to worry. Cats wear their nine lives all at once, layering them like clothes, impenetrable as thick armor.

Everyone wonders what these nine lives might be made of. If you tossed a cat into a sea of knives or an ocean of boiling oil, what would happen? Of course, no one would actually do this, so we can only eye our cats and imagine how it might play out.

Cat lost his first life falling from a tall building. He decided one day to leap from our balcony to the air-conditioning unit but slipped and tumbled down several stories, landing in our little community garden. His outer layer got ripped to shreds by the tree branches as he fell through them. The tatters have probably completely disintegrated by now and are mulching into the soil as we speak.

His second life was lost choking on a bone. Following the aroma of meat, Cat dug into the trash and found a rib. Thinking he'd scored a fleshy treat, Cat gulped it down without even chewing. The bone was too big and got stuck in his throat, leaving him unable to breathe. In agony, Cat thrashed around on the ground, fraying his second garment into nonexistence.

His third life got drowned. One evening, I filled the tub with water for a nice bubble bath. While I wasn't looking, Cat snuck into the bathroom. By the time I found him, his third garment was floating limply on the surface.

As for his fourth life—I'd poured myself a glass of scalding water, and it sat there emitting white vapor. Cat loves drinking from my water glass, and he knows he has to do this swiftly before I stop him. As usual, he came over and took a big gulp. Shocked and in pain from the boiling water, he knocked over the glass and his fourth life evaporated like steam.

Cat's fifth life was lost to illness. He got sick and stopped eating and drinking, while his stomach kept swelling. I brought him to the animal hospital, where the vet said there was nothing she could do. He was in such torment, barely clinging on to life, and the vet suggested putting him to sleep to end his suffering. We left Cat's fifth outfit at the animal hospital, a few fibers of fabric still clinging to the vet's syringe.

Curiosity killed Cat's sixth life. It was just like the proverb, which Cat of course ignored. We'd brought home a huge box, and Cat couldn't rest till he knew what was inside. He wouldn't stop worrying away at it. The box was actually empty—but his expectations had been so heightened that by the time he finally saw that it contained nothing, a cloud of curiosity shrouded him and he refused to believe the truth before his eyes. He spent so long scrabbling around in the box, obsessed with uncovering its secrets, that he wore away his sixth item of clothing.

The seventh life was done in by overeating. The pet store had a sale, so I stocked up on tinned food. Cat had never seen so many cans before, and the variety of flavors so excited him that he insisted on trying every one. He sampled them one after the other, unable to stop gorging until his stomach exploded, taking the seventh garment with it.

Cat got rid of his eighth life on purpose. Having already lost seven lives, Cat couldn't think of any other ways of dying, except deliberately. The way he did this is a secret. No one knows what exactly happened, but he left home and went on a long walk. When he came back, he only had one layer of clothing left.

Cat's ninth life is his final one and no matter what, it clings stubbornly to him. Whatever extremes he goes to, this ninth outfit remains intact, following him everywhere he goes.

Cat came running over, wanting me to help him solve this mystery. I must have run my hands over him at least ten times before I realized: this final life was connected to mine. And because I happen to be in the prime of my life, Cat will also remain very healthy. Cat and I are now both on our final remaining lives, and we'll both have to treat them carefully, as our lives are linked.

40
Cat Balance

Cat loves being on the balcony, frolicking around and lounging in the sun. It's nice out there with plenty of light. An outdoor space with fresh air, daylight, and a view of clouds. Cat's not the only one—I enjoy being out there too.

There are many fun things to explore on the balcony. Cat likes finding breaks in his routine and inventing new games. He'll climb the water pipes more than two meters high, then jump off and execute a perfect landing. I can tell he's into this and feels smug about his abilities. A few days after discovering this trick, I saw him leap onto the railing, which is just two inches wide, and stride across it like a tightrope walker.

Cat's legs crisscrossed with confidence. He moved unhurriedly, showing no fear of falling. Placing his center of gravity in his belly, he proceeded steadily yet vigilantly, every inch the experienced circus artiste.

After a few rounds parading on the balcony railing, Cat's eyes moved from his paws to the cloud before him. Taking a big step forward, then another one, Cat vaulted onto the cloud. With one solid jump and one light skip, he was at its center. It was much more solid here than you might imagine—softer and springier—and he hopped around happily. Fortunately he managed to jump straight up and land back down on the cloud, rather than falling off it.

All this while, I'd been sweating profusely for him, perspiration threatening to engulf my whole forehead.

Cat returned from the clouds, stepping daintily back onto the railing, resuming his own performance. His core seemed more stable now, and his balancing skills were extraordinary, bringing him an endless source of joy. He'd spent less than a minute parading on the railing, but it felt like hours to me, as if we'd been sucked into a black hole and all time had been swallowed too.

When Cat had finally had enough, he settled down onto the railing, his belly bearing his entire weight, limbs suspended in midair, ready for a nap. His claws sank into the cloud layers next to him, which held him up securely. After a lengthy yawn, he covered his face and shut his eyes, and his tail drooped languorously. He was like a gust of wind rolling off the cloud.

I scooped Cat off the railing, waking him. He struggled out of my embrace and ran back to the balcony edge, ready to jump back up. Luckily, I could tell right away what he was planning and managed to move even faster, lunging over to grab hold of him and bundle him indoors. I didn't dare let him have his way on that dangerous balcony.

A few days after this episode, I told Husband to hire someone to fit a panel along the length of the balcony. This huge slab of glass is completely clear—you can barely tell it's there. Cat doesn't seem to have noticed there's now a barrier between him and the open air. He continues jumping onto the railing as before, treading lightly with his cat steps.

41
Cat-Ball Planets

A couple of egglike objects used to dangle from Cat's rump, like a pair of twin planets. They didn't rotate nor did they orbit anything (not even each other), they just moved in whatever direction Cat did: a straight line when he walked straight ahead, swerving when he went zigzag, vaulting to a higher point in the universe when he jumped, and staying still when he was stationary.

Astronomers hadn't gotten round to naming these planets yet, so I took the liberty of calling them the Cat-Ball Planets.

As Cat grew up, these planets grew with him. Soon, they could be seen by people on other planets. When we look up at the night sky, we remember that Earth is just

another celestial body among many others, including the twin Cat-Ball Planets. They reflect sunlight, making use of the sun's excess energy. Cat loved basking in the sun because his planets needed to absorb sufficient heat and light to blaze at night, like bright stars in the sky.

Many of my friends who saw these twin globes praised their roundness and fullness and said how clever Cat was to have sprouted such special planets. They even said these objects were not just well-formed but also a little mysterious, with something ineffable about them. When they were fully grown, they'd surely leave Cat and this home, and travel to the distant cosmos.

I asked when they would leave, but my friends said this was hard to say. They'd make their escape once Cat was fully grown, and there was no going against the course of nature.

A few months after this, Cat began yowling all the time and peeing everywhere. Friends told me this was the clearest sign that the Cat-Ball Planets were ready to make their departure. Cat seemed terribly sad; I guess because he was sorry to see them go.

In the end, I brought Cat to the vet. It took just over ten minutes for the planets to go from Cat's rump to dangling between the vet's fingers. Even then, they were still swaying.

The final step in their escape plan.

A few moments later, the planets disappeared from the building. I glimpsed them heading toward the window, but the vet didn't seem to care—probably she'd seen this happen too many times. Cat was still knocked out, so on his behalf, I observed the planets' departure.

The orbs made a final round through the air, like a farewell. Then they began to ascend, twin spaceships shooting blue laser beams. They were heading for Planet Meow, which my friends tell me is where all cats go when they die.

The pair of cat balls ended up as tiny satellites orbiting Planet Meow. Maybe the smallest objects floating through the vast emptiness of the universe. Their surface started out barren, containing nothing at all except the memory of Cat's scent.

After some time, as they pined for Cat, the Cat-Ball Planets suddenly sprouted a hair. And then a second one, a third, a fourth. . . .

By now, both planets have grown a thick foliage that looks identical to cat fur. And at a certain point, when the appropriate season arrives, these strands will leave the ground, drifting through the void like dandelion fluff.

42
Mysterious Code

Cat's balls might have departed for outer space, but I don't think they've completely cut off contact. They retain Cat's scent and sprout furlike vegetation. The strands that leave these planets behave just like the fur that Cat sheds, dispersing information in all directions. Cat receives these signals and passes them on to me.

Cat frequently jumps onto my desk and walks across my keyboard. He pretends this is by accident, but I know he's leaving coded messages. More than once, he's trodden on certain keys to leave a string of gibberish. When I let him be, he'll come back after a while to tap out another line of symbols. Unfortunately, I'm unable to decipher these messages.

Once, I called Husband over and asked, "Do you know what Cat is saying?" Screwing up his eyes, he carefully looked through the messages, left to right and right to left, making *hmm* noises. Impatiently, I said, "Do you understand cat-writing or not?" He made more thoughtful sounds, then said, "The way I see it, Cat is saying he's hungry and wants something to eat." I rolled my eyes. "Stop bluffing. He's just had some chicken breast. How could he still be hungry?" Husband said under his breath, "He was sent by aliens to punish stupid earthlings like you."

Husband's muttering made me think: Could the symbols tapped out by Cat be messages from outer space? But no, what were the odds that alien beings would be sending me messages via Cat? It's still a matter of debate whether aliens even exist at all. Much more likely these signals were coming from the Cat-Ball Planets. When I told Husband my theory, he chuckled. "What are you talking about? What Cat-Ball Planets? This is clearly the work of aliens!" Waxing eloquent, he began listing all the evidence for his hypothesis: Cat loves being active at night because the humans are asleep, so he can go unobserved to the window and communicate with aliens in the night sky. Every strand of Cat's fur is an antenna that can send or receive messages, and Cat only sheds his fur in order for new transmitters to replace the older ones, constantly upgrading his technology so he remains state of the art. The secret messages sent by the aliens remain in Cat's body, just like the food he eats. He is absorbing all kinds of information, and when he sees a suitable opportunity, such as a human being using her laptop, he'll leap up onto the desk and quickly tap out these messages onto the screen.

Husband's explanation was persuasive, and I couldn't immediately think of a comeback, but I still believed in my intuition: these messages must surely come from the Cat-Ball Planets not from some other unknown species.

I've saved all of Cat's cryptic messages in a folder, and whenever I have a spare moment, I go back to staring at them. Hopefully the day will come when I'm finally able to crack this secret code.

43
Horizon

If Cat wasn't always falling asleep on the windowsill, I'd never have noticed you can see the horizon from this angle. A blurry line where the sky joins the city, shoved into all kinds of strange angles by buildings of different heights. When I squint, it looks close enough for me to pick it up between two fingers, a twisted rubber band that's lost its elasticity and grown stiff.

Cat sprawls on the sill with his eyes almost shut, and I too gaze at him with my eyes narrowed to slits. When he happens to lounge against the horizon, he splays out his body and it looks as if the horizon is buckling beneath him, and the buildings with it. Perhaps it's actually Cat who stretched out the horizon and made it grow slack. He has no idea and doesn't care. At moments like this, Cat is like some strange monster descending from the sky in a Hollywood film, only we've happened to catch the beast at rest. When he awakens, every step he takes will cause massive destruction until the entire city has been flattened.

Cat's chosen sleeping position often happens to be exactly where the sun rises or sets. When he oversleeps, he blocks the sun's path. After a long day at work in the sky, the sun would love to get off the job promptly at six, but when it goes to leave, it finds a fat mound of flesh in its way. Only when Cat wakes up and walks away can the sun finally depart.

Cat isn't always thoughtful enough to allow the sun safe passage. Sometimes he's so lazy that he's unwilling to shift an inch and keeps lying there. As a result, the sun is left waiting around, and daytime is extended a little.

The sun isn't always well-tempered enough to wait patiently either. Finding it can't go home after an exhausting day, its face grows bright red with anger, staining the clouds around it. Affected by the sun's mood, the clouds go from scarlet to purple, and that's why twilight is so colorful, a dazzling display between horizon and sky. As the sky grows incandescent with rage, the entire sky and all

the clouds over the city look like they've been set on fire, a rare sight of flaming clouds overhead.

Everyone in the city looks up at this scene, snapping photos to post online. No one could guess that if they went searching, they'd find that Cat was the source of all this. Cat himself isn't interested in the view though; he'd rather spend the evening snoring away.

But don't think Cat is consistently lazy—there are many occasions when he wakes up even before the sun has begun its descent, once the temperature begins to fall. Cat understands that at this point, not only will he no longer be able to absorb any more sunlight but all the heat he's carefully stored away during the day will dissipate if he stays put. Besides, he'll be getting hungry, so he stands up and walks away, clearing the way for the sun's exit.

This happens most often when winter arrives and it's cold all day. Temperatures plummet even further come evening, and Cat wakes extra early from his nap, afraid of the chill. The sun takes the opportunity to slip away early too, disappearing below the horizon before its usual time. And so in the winter, night lasts much longer.

44
Hairballs

Cat licks his fur all day long on sunny days, rainy days, cloudy days, pretty much all kinds of days, three hundred and sixty-five days per year. A person can go a day without washing her face, but no cat could do without their tongue bath. A cat's tongue serves as both towel and hairbrush, and keeps its owner spic and span, clean and comfortable, making its body more alert. Cats strike all kinds of poses as they lick themselves, showing great flexibility, executing complicated movements to get at those hard-to-reach spots, making sure to get every inch from the gaps between their toes to their bumholes, paying great attention to each cranny. As time goes on, cats accumulate large amounts of fur in their bellies, which they're unable to digest. As a result, they develop hairballs in their guts, which get vomited up from time to time.

A human who chooses to live with a cat will inhale large quantities of fur every day. That builds up inside us too and, over time, forms even larger hairballs.

As more and more cat fur comes together, it gets braided into rope, which then is coiled up, just like the balls of wool my mother used to knit sweaters from back in the day. Everything gets clumped together into a little cat. We unintentionally lick up the fur floating through the air, just like licking a cat. Which is how I came to have a cat named Woolly in my stomach, because I'd ingested the equivalent of a ball of wool.

The little cat hopped around inside me, but she was still unsteady on her feet and fell over, giving me a bit of a tummy ache. It was a charming pain though, and I was willing to put up with it.

I went about my life as usual: eating, sleeping, writing, drawing. Now and then I'd remember the wool in my stomach and smile gleefully to myself. No one knew this secret. No one could tell I had a clump of wool inside me, growing larger by the day, as if I had an actual baby, a child of my own.

No matter where I went, the ball of wool went with me. Now I think about it, that was quite unusual. I distinctly remember hearing the wool rolling this way and that inside me, *grr grr grr*. People probably thought it was my stomach rumbling. None of them could have guessed my secret.

Until the day came when I needed to cough up my hairball.

I was on the couch watching TV with Cat sitting motionless by my side, staring straight at me. He might have sensed what was going on before I did. Having thrown up countless hairballs, a cat is always going to be more experienced than a human who's never done it. And he must have known this moment was coming.

Just as the program came to an end and the credits started rolling, I abruptly barfed up onto the floorboards. It didn't hurt at all but hit me so suddenly I wasn't prepared. And there before me was a round blob of fur, still dripping with stomach juices, sticky to the touch. Cat reached out a paw to tentatively prod it but shrank back before he could make contact. None of us had seen such a large hairball before—it was the size of a two-month-old kitten. An alarmed look came into Cat's eyes, and the same into mine too.

The hairball stirred. A short while later, four legs protruded from the clump, a pair of eyes blinked open, and there was a tender little kitten!

45
Cat and Kitten

Although we should have been psychologically prepared, Kitten's appearance shocked me and Cat. It was unthinkable enough to have spat up such a huge hairball, let alone for it to start moving, to demand food and water, to stumble around as it learned to walk. Feeling threatened, Cat glared warily at the newcomer, and I had to reassure him that Kitten wasn't here to replace him. I wasn't thinking of them as New Cat and Old Cat, only as Cat and Kitten.

Husband hadn't come home yet, so we had the flat to the three of us. Cat stared at Kitten, who stared back at him, and I stared at them both. Just the three of us, existing in the same space and time. I understood very clearly in that moment that I hadn't lost a cat but rather gained one.

I picked up Kitten from the ground to pet her and look at her more closely. She was tiny enough that I could hold her in my palm, even smaller than Cat when I first found him. She was completely silent and felt very light as I held her. Her fur was sparse but very fluffy.

She looked completely innocent, and her eyes were wide with wonder at the world. All of a sudden, I was overjoyed. I held her up to Cat and said, "Look!" Out of nowhere, he leaped into the air and retreated about a meter. I thought I must have moved too abruptly and startled him, but when I very slowly came closer, he kept going backward. I stopped, and he stayed what he regarded as a safe distance away, still eyeing Kitten. I brought her back to the sofa and kept playing with her.

When Husband got home, he was much calmer than me at the sight of Kitten. "We might as well keep her," he said. "It's just as easy to have two cats as one." Besides, we'd already been thinking of getting a kitten: a playmate for Cat, another little friend for us. Now our wish had come true. How marvelous! I explained to him that a hairball had transformed into Kitten, and he said we'd wanted another cat so much she could have transformed out of anything.

That was true. It turns out hairballs don't just look like cats, they actually *are* cats. Every cat is just one big hairball rolling around on the floor.

Cat very quickly came to accept Kitten. To start with, he treated her like a ball of wool, chasing her around or holding her to his chest and worrying at her with his hind paws and teeth, just as he did with his favorite toys. Kitten cried out at this torture but never tried to take revenge. It was as if she had no memory and could forget Cat's nastiness right away. A moment after each incident, she'd go peaceably up to him again, snuggling by his side. She clung to him all day long like glue and refused to be separated.

Eventually, Cat got used to being clung to. Now, when he's wrapped around Kitten, he no longer bites her but rather licks her head over and over again.

46
North and South Poles

Cat is male and Kitten is female. Opposites attract, and it's like Cat is the north pole of a magnet and Kitten is the south pole. They exert a pull on each other.

Kitten is a small magnet while Cat is a large one, which naturally makes him a more powerful force. Most of the time, it will be Cat standing still, and Kitten being drawn to him. This natural attraction is enviable. I often find myself wishing I could be a giant magnet, pulling them both toward me.

Kitten spends her days trotting around behind Cat, as inseparable from him as his shadow. Sometimes I bundle

her away, forcibly keeping them apart, but she'll only spend a couple of minutes in my arms before struggling free and stumbling off to go find Cat. Even standing at her full height, she only comes up to Cat's chest, and snuggles against him the way a bird might nestle against a person. Cat crouches on the ground, not even looking at Kitten, just staring into the middle distance, looking very serious. He wants to seem mature and dignified in front of Kitten, not frivolous at all. However much she clambers on top of him and romps around, he remains unmoved.

Cat might look like a statue, but for all I know, he's secretly been amassing magnetic power. Perhaps it's not Kitten who insists on gamboling all over him, but rather an irresistible force drawing her to his body that she's powerless to escape.

Seeing how besotted Kitten is with Cat, Husband said, not without a tinge of schadenfreude, "What a shame!" I said, "About what?" He replied, "A shame that his balls are gone." Ah! Now I understood what he was saying and felt a burst of relief.

It's lucky for us that Cat's balls have already flown off to orbit Planet Meow by this point. No matter how powerful Cat's magnetism is compared to Kitten's, if those little orbs were still present, the tables would be completely turned, and it would be Cat pursuing Kitten everywhere. How fortunate that Cat's powers of attraction are now pure and simple, with no other agenda or purpose.

When Cat leaps up onto the laundry counter, Kitten is compelled by the magnetic force to follow suit, but she is too small a magnet to have much sway, and despite her small hops and skips, she simply doesn't have the strength to jump so high. All she can do is stare at Cat, her body craning toward him but unable to so much as touch one of his paws.

After she has struggled fruitlessly for ages, Cat will lower his face toward her. Now she can grab on to his head. The two opposing poles are locked together, impossible to separate. She vigorously laps at his forehead fur until he reluctantly jumps off the counter, allowing her to lick her fill.

47
Bodily Odors

Kitten has a sort of milky scent about her, similar to the one that clings to human infants. When she walks past me, she leaves a faint fragrance in the air that grows stronger when I sniff at her.

This aroma has a sweet tang to it and, coupled with Kitten's squishy body, is just as alluring as the White Rabbit milk sweets I ate as a kid. I can't stop sniffing at it, and neither can Cat. Oh, Cat. He's unable to resist drawing close to Kitten, licking her fur, eyes shut, tongue dipping in and out with the same rapture and delight that he laps at his goat milk.

Cat sleeps alongside Kitten, but even with his large body spooning her little one, the milky fragrance still seeps out. It spreads all around, suffusing the air, and when it reaches my nostrils, I seize the opportunity to inhale deeply. This natural and free-floating aroma has a certain unforced wholesomeness. I also like to cuddle Kitten, burying my face in her side, huffing away at her delicious scent. Even if it meant catching Cat Virus, I'd have no regrets.

Cat's body produces odors too, but these are very different from Kitten's. He has no fixed scent but smells different depending on what is wafting through the flat. When we're stewing winter melon with pork ribs, that's what he reeks of. When we're making braised beef, ditto. And when we steam fish with fermented black beans, etc.

Basically, whenever we cook, Cat will start emanating the same culinary scents. Husband will be clattering away in the kitchen, and Cat will squat on the little stool by the entrance, quietly absorbing all the foods' aromas. He gathers all these appetizing smells to himself, then disseminates them far and wide. One sniff of Cat, and I know what to expect for dinner, as if I could part his fur and see a dining table with a delicious spread on it.

When I'm hungry, smelling cat temporarily sates me, just like the men in the old story who satisfied their thirst by gazing at a plum tree. Watching Cat lick himself, watching Kitten lick him, all kinds of weird questions pop into my mind, surprising and amusing me. Is Cat tasty? That probably means Kitten would be delectable too? Haha, I can't help but laugh at my gruesome thoughts.

On any given day, as Cat sprints through the flat, he leaves a trail of aromas, and Kitten comes running after him. Eventually, I realized that Kitten is actually rapt at the delicious smells he gives off, and that's the source of her attraction for him. So I've solved the riddle: it turns out Kitten is nothing more than a greedy guts!

48
Fort of Tangerines

It's been an irrefutable truth for a while now that Cat likes his food, and Kitten has gradually revealed a tendency toward greediness too, just as great if not greater than his. Now that one greedy cat has become two, every meal in our house is chaotic. No sooner is food on the table than the cats will come rushing over to investigate, before we've even had a chance to sit down.

Back when Husband and I only had to deal with Cat, it was two-against-one, so we could just about keep him at bay. Now there are as many cats as people, and it's a full-time job trying to eat our food while fending off the cats from our piping-hot dishes.

Neither Husband nor I can bear to banish the kitties to the balcony, from where they'll stare at us and mew pathetically. Whenever we try that, Husband's heart always softens and he lets them back in before long. We regret our kindness every single time—the price we pay is for the meal to become a battleground. And yet we can't help ourselves, even though we're the ones who end up suffering in the end.

During tangerine season, Husband brought home a large bag of the fruit and left it on the table. That evening, dinnertime rolled around, yet there was no sign of the cats arriving for their daily siege. What was going on?

Just as we were speculating why the cats hadn't shown up as usual, Cat couldn't resist the lure of the succulent aromas and jumped onto the table. My heart sank. Here it was, the moment when mealtime turned into wartime. I prepared to do battle.

Yet strangely, although Cat had breached the table, he wasn't sniffing around our plates as usual. Instead, he perched in one corner, separated from us by that bag of tangerines.

Husband put down his chopsticks and reached out for a tangerine, which he held right in front of Cat's nose.

Cat's face scrunched up instantly, and he began warily retreating. I grabbed another tangerine and thrust it at Kitten, who reacted similarly: looking terrified and beating a hasty retreat.

As so, through sheer chance, we now know the one thing that repels the cats. As long as there are tangerines on the table, they don't dare encroach. Husband and I were so overjoyed at this revelation, you'd think we were explorers who'd discovered a new continent. From that point on, we've been able to eat in peace.

Tangerines are now a regular presence in our home. Husband brings home bag after bag of them, weapons for our arsenal in the war against the kitties. If they dare to leap onto the table, we build forts of tangerines around them, a big one for Cat and a little one for Kitten, encircling them both separately, leaving them unable to take a single step. It's as if we've cast a spell on them, as if the air around them has solidified. Not only do they not cause any more mischief, but they sit there obediently as if they're our attendants, watching motionless as Husband and I eat our food.

49
Alarm Clock

Beep beep beep. That's the alarm clock. Time to get up.

That's a sound from my past, though. I'm not sure exactly when this began, but our alarm clock rarely has a chance to go off these days. Rather, it's now the kitties who jump onto the bed and meow into our ears nonstop. My eyes blink open, then droop shut again. Open, close. Over and over, until I drop off again. Seeing I have no intention of getting up, the cats bring out the big guns: Cat licks my face, while Kitten licks my feet, tickling me at both ends. I thrash my legs and shake my head, but this dispels the last of my drowsiness, and I am forced out of bed. Having got their way, the kitties twine delightedly between my legs. I have to admit that this very paws-on

method of waking me is far more effective than the alarm clock ever was—it only ever produced a loud sound. Not that the cat-alarms are silent, they just go *meow meow meow* instead of *beep beep beep*.

The first time this happened, the kitties summoned me out of bed and led me to their empty bowls. Seeing that not one speck of food was left, I understood why they'd woken me with such urgency, and hurried to fill the bowls. Petting their heads, I told them, "Go ahead, eat!" Then I went to the kitchen to get something for myself. Lazybones that I am, it had been a while since I'd been up in time for breakfast.

The following day, I was awakened again, and this time

they brought me to the window. Looking outside, I saw the sun just appearing in the gaps between the buildings, swaggering up into the sky, all puffed up and growing larger, anxious that the sharp-edged skyscrapers might puncture it. As the sun carefully rose, its crimson glow dyed the surrounding clouds with a delicate blush. It had been a while, I realized, since I'd seen the dawn.

On day three, the kitties led me from the bed to my desk. In the middle was a new book I hadn't even unwrapped yet—even though I'd bought it a whole week ago. I'd wasted so much time that week having fun. How long had it been since I'd settled down to read a good book?

The fourth, fifth, and sixth days followed. Now we're at the nth day—I've lost count. And still the kitties spring to me each morning, waking me up on time. *Meow meow meow . . . meow meow meow. . . .* That's the alarm clock. Time to get up.

50
Dissolving

I had a cold. Headache, cough, runny nose, the works. My doctor prescribed a very bitter medicine. Just as I morosely geared up to take my next dose, Kitten decided to have a sip of the hot water I'd poured myself. She couldn't get her snout into the glass, so she reached in to scoop some out. No sooner had her paw touched the water than it dissolved like salt, followed quickly by the rest of Kitten.

Cat and I were frantic at Kitten's disappearance. We stared at the completely clear glass of hot water, not knowing what to do. Cat quickly picked out Kitten's scent in the water and jumped onto the table to investigate further. Bringing his nose close to the glass, he confirmed that it was indeed Kitten he was smelling. He leaned in to lap at the water, but as soon as his tongue made contact with the surface, he went the same way as Kitten, melting without warning.

Having witnessed Cat and Kitten dissolve before my eyes, I gaped as if I'd seen a magic trick close up. This was completely unbelievable. No time to figure out how this had happened. I quickly lifted the glass and studied it. Where had my kitties gone? That was the only question on my mind.

The cats were gone. The volume of water in the glass remained exactly the same, and it looked like regular water but smelled different: an acrid, botanical reek that was growing stronger, not dissimilar to my cold medicine.

I shouted into the glass but got no response. All I saw was a slice of my own face reflected on the surface. I pinched my nose and glugged down the entire glass. Right away, my taste buds screamed that this tasted bad, and I stuck out my tongue, feeling my features contort. At the same moment, coziness flowed through my gut, and there was heat in my chest too, as if I was embracing both kitties and their warmth was spreading throughout my entire body.

I kept calling their names, but still there was no answer. Before long, a strange weariness overtook me, and my eyes drifted shut. Lying down on the sofa, I fell asleep.

By the time I woke up, the sky was dark, and city lights were glinting through the thin cloud cover. How had I slept so long? I sat up and felt quite a bit lighter, and my headache was better than before. The kitties ran out from who knows where, coming over and begging to be petted. I felt them both all over and found them whole. I stroked Cat, then Kitten. Both were solid, not changed in the slightest.

The water glass stood on the table, also unchanged, empty.

51
Picking Mushrooms

Come on, friends, let's forage for mushrooms! No need to leave the house, and no need to wait for spring. In my home, plenty of mushrooms sprout each day. Here's one on the sofa, and here's one on the floor, and the coffee table, and the bed . . . for all seasons, for all weather.

I don't live in a forest nor am I near any body of water that could make the flat damp, yet these mushrooms grow large and plump, each of them nicely round, fuzzy with a clear pattern. They pop up everywhere around me all the time and spring into being fully mature, no need to wait for them to grow. Come pick a mushroom or two; don't hesitate; they sprout quickly and disappear quickly too. A moment's inattention, and a mushroom you had your eye on could vanish just like that.

There's a mushroom on the bookcase, but turn your back for a moment and it could go away. That happens all the time. Then later, an identical specimen sprouts on the chair. They're everywhere, large and small, covered in fuzz, coarse or fine, long or short. The big ones look meaty and solid, promising to be chewy. The small ones are so delicate they're sure to melt in your mouth.

Come along, we're going mushroom picking. Get a nice tender one to make into soup, that'll be delicious. Oh yes, even a single mushroom can make an abundant meal.

You don't need any equipment to gather mushrooms. The sun isn't going to burn you; the rain isn't going to drench your clothes. No need to pick your way through thick grass, no need to be frightened of whatever snakes or bugs might be lurking in the undergrowth. There's no effort involved; we're just seeking out mushrooms amid our furniture.

But where are the mushrooms? Why is it that, just as we've set out to pick them, all the mushrooms have gone away? No big ones, no little ones. How strange.

Not to worry. The mushrooms have probably found somewhere new to sprout. That's how it is—they enjoy being in different places, and no sooner have they gotten used to one spot than they'll move to another.

These mushrooms have grown legs, so they can walk wherever they want.

They don't grow outside though. Just search every cranny of the flat carefully, and you're sure to find a mushroom. There we go! After just a bit of searching, there are a couple of mushrooms under the bed, newly sprouted from the look of them. So fresh: a big one and a little one, huddled close together. A few strands of fur float through the air, barely visible.

Delighted, I pluck them both. That should provide a few days' worth of delicious meals. Lying belly down on the floor, I reach in and easily grab hold of the big mushroom. I'm all excited, but then the little mushroom disappears just like that. Never mind, I have the big one. We'll leave the small one for another day.

52
Catsup

One afternoon, having nothing better to do, I decided to see what would happen if I mixed Cat and Kitten together. As I stirred away, something miraculous happened: There was a chemical reaction between the kitties. They softened, losing their shapes, melting from solid to liquid and slowly blending together until I had a pot of sticky catsup. This sauce was a shade in between their coat colors, one that could only be formed by combining different dyes. A little darker than Cat's fur, a little paler than Kitten's. A solid gray, like sesame paste.

After being mixed, the catsup emitted a strong fragrance, also rather like sesame paste, irresistible. Luckily, since this pot of sauce consisted of the two greedy kitties,

I could be sure they wouldn't come along to disturb me. Unable to stop myself, I dipped a finger in and touched it to my tongue. Immediately, a delicious flavor filled my mouth. It was completely captivating, unlike anything I'd ever tasted before. Out of all the many adjectives used to describe food, I couldn't think of a single one that would be fitting. The catsup was simply so tasty one mouthful wasn't enough. I went to the kitchen for a bowl and spoon, and quickly gobbled down several bowlfuls. No matter how much I ate, the supply of catsup remained inexhaustible. It was because the kitties hadn't actually gone away, you see. As long as they were still around, there would never be any shortage of catsup.

The catsup wasn't just for eating either. It also worked beautifully as a skin cream, as a healing lotion, as wall plaster. . . . When I applied it to my face, it was quickly absorbed and felt much more soothing than my usual expensive skincare products. My complexion was smooth and clear afterward with a faint, lingering fragrance.

After the cats transformed into catsup, they had to move around differently. No longer could they walk or jump on four legs to get where they needed to be. Catsup could only be spread, which meant they had to spread themselves to get places. This had the effect of expanding their range of motion quite a lot. For instance, they didn't used to be able to climb walls, but catsup can easily be smeared on a wall. Watching this, you could imagine the kitties bouncing off walls and vaulting onto rooftops like warriors in a wuxia film. Once they were on the wall, they'd stay up there for several hours, long enough for a blissful nap.

Since that day, I haven't needed to mix the kitties; they turn into catsup all on their own. When I'm not paying attention, I'll suddenly find sauce spattered everywhere. For some reason, a lot of it seems to end up on the ceiling. Maybe it's because they sneeze quite vigorously, or maybe they just can't stand peace and quiet so they send catsup splashing everywhere, turning the entire place into their playground.

53
Extreme Sports

Cat is really quite buff. As he strides around, you can see the definition of his muscles, clearly highlighting his strapping physique, as if he's just emerged from a gym. No question about it, his gym is our flat. And now Cat has taught Kitten how to turn our home into a fitness center, a place in which all kinds of death-defying extreme sports can take place.

Cat's favorite activity is parkour. The way furniture of different heights is laid out in our home happens to be perfectly suited for this. Kitten, being much smaller, isn't able to jump as high and can't come close to matching his prowess. And so Cat jumps alone from the top of one cabinet to another, moving with speed and precision with an awesome variety of postures. Husband and I watch with our hearts in our mouths. We're not worried that Cat will slip and hurt himself, more that he will knock over the vases or glassware in the cabinets. This has happened more than once: Cat sending an ornament I particularly liked crashing to the ground, where it shatters into tiny pieces, as does my heart.

Cat feels no shame about these incidents—in fact, he's proud of them. Whenever he reaches a spot that's particularly difficult to get to, he'll perch there for a while, gazing down at me with a look of superiority, the unmistakable air of a champion.

What with his innate sense of control and balance, Cat was born to be a parkour star. I've never seen him miss his footing. Occasionally, human beings get pulled into his obstacle course: Husband and I find our bodies being treated no differently than wardrobes or chairs. We'll be sitting on the couch or asleep in bed, completely unprepared, when the kitties suddenly spring onto our bellies or chests, inevitably Cat followed by Kitten, a one-two punch, heavy followed by light. Before I even have a chance to cry out "aiyoh," the kitties will have made their escape.

Kitten may not be as good as Cat at parkour, but she can more than hold her own in drag racing. The two of them turn the smooth tiled surface of our living room floor into a racetrack with their own bodies for cars, their legs turning into wheels. Having marked out their course, they'll pretend to be chasing each other and playing around as usual, all the while charging straight ahead, one behind the other. Halfway down the living room, their legs stop moving and momentum alone carries them forward round a bend in a perfect C-shaped arc. Then they race back to the finish line for more speeding, cornering, drifting.

Cat and Kitten have so much fun that I can't help but join in. I'll grab a sheet of tissue paper, wad it up into a ball, and fling it from one end of the living room. The three of us go chasing after it, slipping and sliding across the floor. No matter how many rounds we play of this game, I always come in last.

54
Massage Parlor

Cat and Kitten have another shared interest: they love massaging objects. Blankets, pillows, mattresses, armchairs, you name it. Their front paws alternate up and down, padding down on the softness beneath, sheer bliss. Husband and I often find ourselves receiving massages too. When they first did this, the kitties stood so upright, looking so professional. We could see they were clearly ready to set up their own shop. This massage parlor would have no sign and would never advertise.

When Cat was alone and working solo, the services he offered were limited without much variation. By the time he'd finished massaging me and moved on to my husband, he'd look a bit tired and much less enthusiastic. Since Kit-

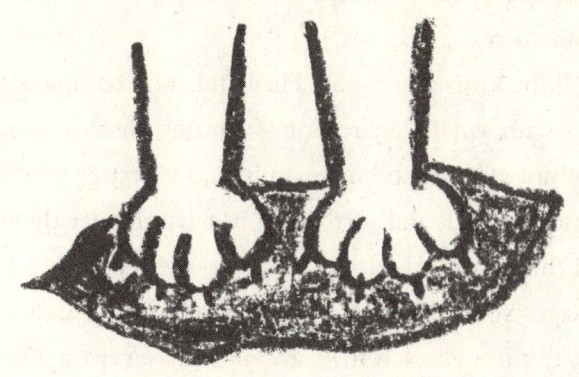

ten's arrival, they've been able to work on us one-to-one. Therefore, they're ready to open their store.

On the day of the grand opening, Husband and I lounged on the couch, enjoying our VIP experience. Cat and Kitten stood on our thighs, looking for all the world like a pair of fully trained masseurs. Their forelegs went up and down, claws spread wide, rhythmically kneading away. The kitties' eyes were narrowed, and their mouths emitted soft *purr purr purrs*. They appeared to be having an even better time than their clients. Now and then, their claws would pierce our trousers and dig into flesh, which felt like an ant bite. This sting of pain was their acupuncture.

All the kitties ask is that Husband and I completely go along with what they're doing. During these massages, we're not allowed to budge an inch, no matter how they trample us back and forth—we just have to let them do what they want. Above all, when you're receiving a kitty massage, you absolutely cannot abandon the treatment halfway through or refuse any of their services. The cat massage parlor is a very powerful institution, where customers have no rights whatsoever. It's basically one of those sinister taverns from old movies where villains conspire, and unsuspecting visitors get their throats slit. As soon as you step inside, you're at the mercy of the kitties. They work whatever hours they decide, and each massage lasts as long as they feel. When I think about it, I'm not sure whether they're at our service, or if it's actually the other way round.

To be honest, I'm increasingly certain that the true purpose of the massage parlor is to satisfy the cats' need to knead. The true customers here are the kitties themselves. Husband explained to me that cats love pressing their paws into soft objects because it stirs up kittenhood memories of massaging their mothers' teats as they suckled in order to stimulate the release of milk.

Without realizing it, Husband and I seem to have stepped into a trap set by the kitties. It's too late for regrets now. Fortunately, we aren't the only things they massage—they also have to service all the other soft objects around, which they lay into with just as much energy and enjoyment, *purr purr purr*. And just like that, the massage parlor has become a bustling business, and the kitties have their paws full.

55
Stuck

The kitties keep getting stuck.

First Cat gets stuck, then Kitten gets stuck, and next it's both. Sometimes they're stuck in different places, sometimes the same one.

When the cats are stuck, they remain completely inert, eyes unblinking, expressions calm, not meowing to be rescued but looking unhappy when a human comes close.

Quick, get out of here! Their dead-eyed stares warns us.

The kitties get stuck in all kinds of places, perhaps just wide enough for them to squeeze into, perhaps slightly too narrow for their bodies—no larger, anyway. They make sure to cram into each location at least once, shrinking their bodies into all sorts of shapes.

If one of them is pressed into a corner, they'll become triangular. If a cardboard box, rectangular. If a bowl, round.

Sometimes Kitten gets stuck in Cat, while Cat is stuck in one of his favorite spots. They can stay like that a very long time, looking like a naturally occurring mortise and tenon, able to slot together perfectly whenever they want.

The kitties are always pressing themselves against each other, and while stuck in this position, they sometimes nap or daydream. Cats enjoy the sensation of being squashed. If they were able, they'd like to wedge themselves into Husband or me, between our fingers or in the gaps in our teeth. How else can you explain the way, when I spread my fingers and sink them into their fur, pushing into their flesh, they contentedly go *purr purr purr*.

Even more often, the kitties get stuck in a sunbeam. Anywhere with enough light and heat, they'll jam themselves into, adjust their positions, and make sure the glow gets 360 degrees all around them. At these moments, the shape they take on is a halo, a pure shimmering radiance that you can only look upon from a distance; otherwise, the brightness would ruin your eyes.

The cats also get stuck in delicious aromas: wet or dry cat food, bonito flakes, cat jelly, catnip. Once they get their heads stuck into the scents of these tasty treats, they can't be plucked free no matter what.

56
Blossoming

When Cat and Kitten rambunctiously chase each other through the flat, they leave paw prints on every available surface. I'll bring in a white shirt from the laundry line, and before I've had a chance to fold it and place it in the closet, they'll thunder past, leaving prints like plum blossoms, large ones and little ones, delicate and well-formed. I end up staring at these flowers for a long time, appreciating their beauty, forgetting that my clothes are now soiled.

It does mean I'll need to do the laundry all over again. Luckily, we have a washing machine, so I won't have to scrub at it manually—I'm not sure I'd be able to bring myself to disintegrate these adorable flower petals with my own hands.

These plum blossoms flourish everywhere in the flat, though mostly on the white walls. Some come still attached to their branches: the scratches left behind by errant claws, deep and straight, firmly etched in. The kitties say, *Let the flowers bloom*, and bloom they do. It barely takes them any effort nor do they need to use their magic—and it's a starker transformation than the change of seasons. After all, there is only one winter every year, but the kitties are a daily presence. The flowers they bring into being do not need to wait for a particular temperature or time of year.

These kitty plum blossoms are quite different from the ones produced by nature. They come in various shades of murky gray, haphazardly arranged, giving off the scent of cat, unassuming as befits the personality of the plum blossom.

Wherever there are kitties, there will be plum blossoms. Even the air itself is thick with the shade of these flowers, there but not there, the most unobtrusive of blooms barely visible to the human eye. All you can do is wait for them to fall, and sweep up a heap of plum blossom petals, which will already be crumbling to dust.

And yet, among each crop of flowers, there number a few particularly tenacious stragglers that stubbornly refuse to fall. They're clearly different from all the others: tender and pink with sturdier petals, not crumbling to the touch. These ones bloom on the kitties' paws, and they're the best shaped with the purest color. All the other plum blossoms are envious of them.

57
Filtered

There was a murder in the apartment complex next door. Not satisfied with just killing, the culprit also set fire to a flat. I only knew about this when I saw it on the news the next day—it was a major case. Putting down my phone, I sat on the windowsill and sighed sadly, my eyes drifting against my will in the direction of the neighboring compound and gazing at the blackened building. Apparently, the flames had spread quickly, burning several flats above and below the victim's. No wonder the kitties had been so engrossed at the window the night before. I'd wondered what they were staring at.

I looked out for a long time but didn't manage to see anything. Too many buildings, too many trees, too many

people—blocking my vision, hiding the truth. The kitties sat by my side, watching me peering out, and peering out themselves. "What do you think you're staring at?" I said to them. "The human world is too cruel. You're better off being cats." I was just venting—I was so full of rage and fear when I said those words.

I sat alone for a very long time, my heart heavy. The sky was gloomy and gray, thoroughly depressing. The cats stretched out and rolled around on the floor, licking each other. Not a thought in their heads. That's how they went about every single day, apparently free of all worries.

After seeing the inferno, the kitties had flames in their eyes, along with some ash. When I wiped away the gunk around their eyes, I noticed it was black—probably congealed soot. Despite having witnessed a murder, they did not seem afraid. Cats have a filter in their eyes that sieves out these cruel, vicious scenes; one that is also able to block out the darkness of humanity.

In this way, cats are able to preserve their innocence, in stark contrast to people. The more humans live through, the more complicated ideas we have, creating tangles of thought, leading to despair and disappointment. Cats simply filter out all this extraneous matter. They have no need for complexity or depth—those are useless. They understand much better than us how not to overburden themselves but to live lightly.

58
Cats Are Gods

The supreme being is not Buddha nor is it Jehovah. Rather, it is The Cat who reigns over us all. Not that The Cat has any truck with religion, They are not interested in corralling human beings and making us worship some kind of amorphous, illusory thing. The Cat simply hovers above us, observing the mass of living things as loftily as any deity.

The Cat has long dismissed religion as merely an invention of fragile humankind, a spiritual crutch without which civilization could not continue. The Cat sauntered down from Their altar and climbed up a tree, which might not be as high as an altar, but cradled in its branches, The Cat lives with such ease, in sheer delight. As for the busy

insects and humans scurrying around beneath, The Cat is content to simply gaze down upon them.

With Their gleaming eyes, as brilliant as the sun, The Cat watches the bustle below. Ordinary folk go about their day with absolutely no awareness of the god watching them from the treetops. These regular people walk by, gossiping about this or that, digging their noses, spitting on the ground, doing all kinds of inconsequential things, and The Cat sees all. Yet They never express their judgment nor do They give commands—in fact, They're happy to let everyone forget about Their existence entirely. The Cat is so carefree and at ease They have even shrugged off and tossed away the cross borne by the human god for so long.

At one point, The Cat leaped down from the tree and fractured into countless kitties. Some of them climbed other trees or onto rooftops, becoming deities in their own right. Two clambered onto the top of my wardrobe and are now my Cat and Kitten.

My kitties love a high vantage point from which they can see everything, no corner escaping their gaze. Their eyes are four cameras, sometimes pointing in different directions, sometimes in the same one, their 3-D surveillance covering the entire flat—what we might call a god's-eye view. Everything in our home, including each item of furniture, including Husband and me, is utterly visible to the cats. It seems our kitties are our gods, and I silently pray for their continued protection.

59
Pillow and Blanket

As someone who doesn't work in an office, I find myself needing many naps to get through the day, probably just as many naps as the kitties. I don't see this as something to be ashamed of, nor do I think it makes me a useless person; it's just how my life is. I've made my peace with it and allow snoozing to take up a large chunk of my time.

Every afternoon, I grow drowsy soon after lunch. I didn't use to nap, but these days I drop off each afternoon right on schedule. A person's biological clock influences them much more than any timetable devised by humans. As soon as I lie down on the sofa and grow still, the kitties know it's time to come over and prepare for bed. Their naps last much longer than mine—they generally don't wake up till sunset, whereas I rarely sleep much more than an hour. After this time, a pair of tweezers extends from my biological clock—like something in a cartoon—and tugs my eyelids open, at which point I have no choice but to be awake.

When I open my eyes each day, I find myself with a Cat-pillow and Kitten-blanket. They'll remain completely stationary, so immobile you might mistake them for stuffed animals. For a moment, I'll mistake them for an actual pillow and blanket.

Cat is plump and solidly built, particularly around the belly, which has just the right combination of softness and bounce—he's very comfortable to lie against. As for Kitten, her long fur is so luxuriant she feels like the softest of silken quilts, able to keep away any hint of cold. Whenever they're pressed against a human, they'll purr rhythmically, hypnotically. With one of them by my ear and the other on my chest, they add drowsiness to my drowsiness.

This pillow and blanket set don't need cleaning. Bed-linen is never quite the same after laundering, and cotton in particular wears out with each wash, needing to be replaced after just a few years. By contrast, Cat and Kitten can be used again and again, and they'll remain just as soft

and warm as ever, better than new. If they happen to get grubby, they know how to lick themselves clean. They shed fur, but new fur grows back in. All of this is determined by their moods though. Whenever they don't feel like being a pillow and blanket, I don't dare force them. If I annoy them, they'll turn into a saw blade and nails instead, hammering away at my body, and it's not unusual for me to come away battered and covered in wounds.

60
Two People, Two Cats

Two people, two cats, living together: the ideal family unit. The cats play with each other, and so do the people. The cats and humans can play together too. In a home with only one cat, the cat gets clingy and sticks too closely to the human. And one-person households have the same issue, except it's the human who gets too dependent on the cat.

Imagine another cat springing up between the first cat and human, and likewise, another person appearing. A second cat and human showing up at the same time. How joyous for the cat to have another of his kind, how thrilled the human is to see someone else!

At this very moment, Cat and Kitten are going *meow meow* at each other, and I'm chatting with Husband. Never again will our home have only one type of voice in it. Very often, Husband and I will each be hugging a cat, and we'll bring their faces close together, so they can have a meow-conversation or lick each other while we speak looking into each other's eyes, passing emotions back and forth. While this is happening, we'll also be stroking the kitties nonstop, as if we're touching each other. The cats go *purr purr purr*, and everyone falls into a moment of absolute tenderness and comfort.

When I go out, I no longer have to worry about leaving behind a solo cat to get lonely, waiting all alone for his human to get home. The moment I open the front door on my return, I'll see both kitties sprawled on the table closest to the door, staring in my direction.

Even though there are now two cats waiting instead of one, the wait itself is much less arduous. A lone cat has to spend a lot of energy to make time pass, while a second cat can take on half the burden of time, so the two of them feel much less anxious. With another cat to share the long hours, even if the humans don't get home till late, waiting for them is so much easier.

As for Husband and me, when we go out together, we can also split the load of worrying about the kitties, with each of us shouldering half the tension. It really does make a difference—the weight of worry isn't as heavy as before, and I feel much lighter when I'm out and about.

Then we get home, and there are two people, two cats, eight eyes meeting one another. In that moment, loneliness and worry vanish instantly. The good thing is, even when we do have to deal with these difficult matters, they don't take up as much energy or cause as much sadness as before.

So here we are, each human embracing a cat. From the moment we reunite, we are two people, two cats, once again living together in warm coexistence. Four of us, exactly the right number, depending on one another.

Translator's Note Cat

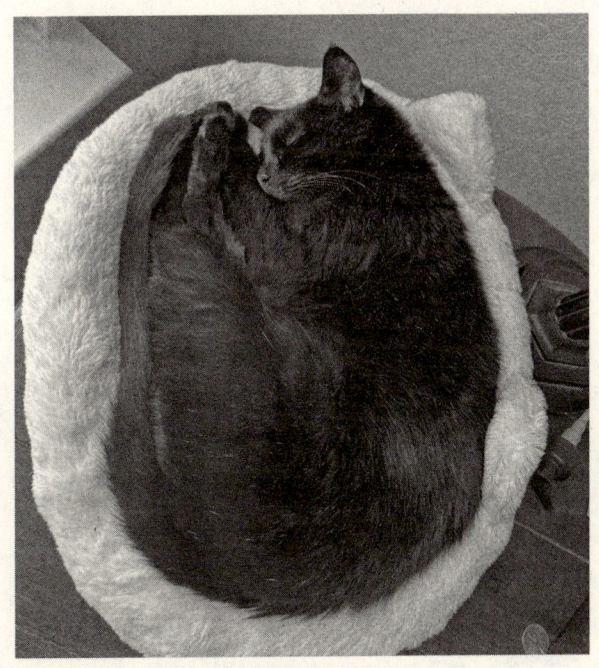

About the Author

Born in 1990, Sichuanese poet Yu Yoyo had already begun to earn critical attention before she turned sixteen, publishing dozens of poems in *Poetry*, *Poetry Monthly*, and other prestigious publications in China.

She studied business management and accounting in university, but she never gave up on her long-standing passion for poetry and finally embraced her life's calling upon graduation. She is now seen as a representative voice among the post-'90s generation and is especially known for her mature voice and subtle treatment of modern femininity.

Her poems have been translated into English, Korean, Russian, French, Japanese, and Swedish. Yoyo has published the following collections in China: *Seven Years* (2012), *Me as Bait* (2016), *Wind Can't* (2019), and *Against Body* (2019). Her latest poetry collection, *Cat Is a Piece of*

Cloud, in memory of one of her cats, was published in 2021. Her first English collection, *My Tenantless Body*, was published by the Poetry Translation Centre in 2019.

Invisible Kitties, originally published in 2021, is her first novel, and its translation rights have been sold to the US, UK, Germany, and Italy. The English editions of *Invisible Kitties*, translated by Jeremy Tiang, will be published by Fourth Estate and HarperVia at the end of 2024. Yu Yoyo is an interdisciplinary artist. Her artistic creation involves writing, drawing, music, photography, and cinema.